John Townsend Trowbridge

The Vagabonds

And other Poems

John Townsend Trowbridge

The Vagabonds
And other Poems

ISBN/EAN: 9783744769976

Printed in Europe, USA, Canada, Australia, Japan

Cover: Foto ©Andreas Hilbeck / pixelio.de

More available books at **www.hansebooks.com**

THE VAGABONDS,

AND OTHER POEMS.

BY

JOHN TOWNSEND TROWBRIDGE.

BOSTON:

JAMES R. OSGOOD AND COMPANY,

LATE TICKNOR & FIELDS, AND FIELDS, OSGOOD, & CO.

1875.

CONTENTS.

LYRICS OF THE WAR.

LIGHTER PIECES.

THE VAGABONDS.

WE are two travellers, Roger and I.
  Roger 's my dog. — Come here, you scamp!
Jump for the gentlemen, — mind your eye!
  Over the table, — look out for the lamp! —
The rogue is growing a little old;
  Five years we 've tramped through wind and weather,
And slept out-doors when nights were cold,
  And ate and drank — and starved — together.

We 've learned what comfort is, I tell you!
  A bed on the floor, a bit of rosin,
A fire to thaw our thumbs (poor fellow!
  The paw he holds up there 's been frozen),
Plenty of catgut for my fiddle
  (This out-door business is bad for strings),
Then a few nice buckwheats hot from the griddle,
  And Roger and I set up for kings!

No, thank ye, Sir, — I never drink;
   Roger and I are exceedingly moral, —
Are n't we, Roger? — See him wink! —
   Well, something hot, then, — we won't quarrel.
He 's thirsty, too, — see him nod his head?
   What a pity, Sir, that dogs can't talk!
He understands every word that 's said, —
   And he knows good milk from water-and-chalk.

The truth is, Sir, now I reflect,
   I 've been so sadly given to grog,
I wonder I 've not lost the respect
   (Here 's to you, Sir!) even of my dog.
But he sticks by, through thick and thin;
   And this old coat, with its empty pockets,
And rags that smell of tobacco and gin,
   He 'll follow while he has eyes in his sockets.

There is n't another creature living
   Would do it, and prove, through every disaster,
So fond, so faithful, and so forgiving,
   To such a miserable, thankless master!

No, Sir! — see him wag his tail and grin!
 By George! it makes my old eyes water!
That is, there 's something in this gin
 That chokes a fellow. But no matter!

We 'll have some music, if you 're willing,
 And Roger (hem! what a plague a cough is, Sir!)
Shall march a little — Start, you villain!
 Paws up! Eyes front! Salute your officer!
'Bout face! Attention! Take your rifle!
 (Some dogs have arms, you see!) Now hold your
Cap while the gentlemen give a trifle,
 To aid a poor old patriot soldier!

March! Halt! Now show how the rebel shakes
 When he stands up to hear his sentence.
Now tell us how many drams it takes
 To honor a jolly new acquaintance.
Five yelps, — that 's five; he 's mighty knowing!
 The night 's before us, fill the glasses! —
Quick, Sir! I 'm ill, — my brain is going! —
 Some brandy, — thank you, — there! — it passes!

Why not reform? That 's easily said;
  But I 've gone through such wretched treatment,
Sometimes forgetting the taste of bread,
  And scarce remembering what meat meant,
That my poor stomach 's past reform;
  And there are times when, mad with thinking,
I 'd sell out heaven for something warm
  To prop a horrible inward sinking.

Is there a way to forget to think?
  At your age, Sir, home, fortune, friends,
A dear girl's love, — but I took to drink; —
  The same old story; you know how it ends.
If you could have seen these classic features, —
  You need n't laugh, Sir; they were not then
Such a burning libel on God's creatures:
  I was one of your handsome men!

If you had seen HER, so fair and young,
  Whose head was happy on this breast!
If you could have heard the songs I sung
  When the wine went round, you wouldn't have guessed

That ever I, Sir, should be straying
    From door to door, with fiddle and dog,
Ragged and penniless, and playing
    To you to-night for a glass of grog!

She 's married since, — a parson's wife:
    'T was better for her that we should part, —
Better the soberest, prosiest life
    Than a blasted home and a broken heart.
I have seen her? Once: I was weak and spent
    On the dusty road: a carriage stopped:
But little she dreamed, as on she went,
    Who kissed the coin that her fingers dropped!

You 've set me talking, Sir; I 'm sorry;
    It makes me wild to think of the change!
What do you care for a beggar's story?
    Is it amusing? you find it strange?
I had a mother so proud of me!
    'T was well she died before — Do you know
If the happy spirits in heaven can see
    The ruin and wretchedness here below?

Another glass, and strong, to deaden
  This pain; then Roger and I will start.
I wonder, has he such a lumpish, leaden,
  Aching thing in place of a heart?
He is sad sometimes, and would weep, if he could,
  No doubt, remembering things that were, —
A virtuous kennel, with plenty of food,
  And himself a sober, respectable cur.

I 'm better now; that glass was warming. —
  You rascal! limber your lazy feet!
We must be fiddling and performing
  For supper and bed, or starve in the street. —
Not a very gay life to lead, you think?
  But soon we shall go where lodgings are free,
And the sleepers need neither victuals nor drink; —
  The sooner, the better for Roger and me!

THE FROZEN HARBOR.

WHEN Winter encamps on our borders,
    And dips his white beard in the rills,
And lays his broad shield over highway and field,
    And pitches his tents on the hills, —
In the wan light I wake, and see on the lake,
    Like a glove by the night-winds blown,
With fingers that crook up creek and brook,
    His shining gauntlet thrown.

Then over the lonely harbor,
    In the quiet and deadly cold
Of a single night, when only the bright,
    Cold constellations behold,
Without trestle or beam, without mortise or seam,
    Is swiftly and silently spread
A bridge as of steel, which a Titan's heel
    In the early light might tread.

Where Morning over the waters
    Her net of splendor spun,
Till the web, all a-twinkle with ripple and wrinkle,
    Hung shimmering in the sun, —
Where the liquid lip at the breast of the ship
    Whispered and laughed and kissed,
And the long, dark streamer of smoke from the steamer
    Trailed off in the rose-tinted mist, —

Now all is gray desolation,
    As up from the hoary coast,
Over snow-fields and islands her white arms in silence
    Outspreading like a ghost,
Her feet in shroud, her forehead in cloud,
    Pale walks the sheeted Dawn :
The sea's blue rim lies shorn and dim,
    In the purple East withdrawn.

Where floated the fleets of commerce,
    With proud breasts cleaving the tide, —
Like emmet or bug with its burden, the tug
    Hither and thither plied, —

Where the quick paddles flashed, where the dropped
    anchor plashed,
    And rattled the running chain,
Where the merchantman swung in the current, where
    sung
    The sailors their far refrain, —

Behold! when ruddy Aurora
    Peeps from her opening door,
Faint gleams of the sun like fairies run
    And sport on a crystal floor;
Upon the river's bright panoply quivers
    The noon's resplendent lance;
And by night through the narrows the moon's slanted
    arrows
    Icily sparkle and glance.

Flown are the flocks of commerce,
    Like wild swans hurrying south;
The coaster, belated, is frozen, full-freighted,
    Within the harbor's mouth;

The brigantine, homeward bringing
　　Sweet spices from **afar,**
All night must wait with her fragrant freight
　　Below the lighthouse star.

The ships at their anchors are frozen,
　　From rudder **to sloping chain :**
Rock-like they **rise : the low sloop lies**
　　An oasis **in the plain.**
Like reeds **here and there, the tall masts bare**
　　Upspring : as **on the** edge
Of a lawn smooth-shaven, around **the haven**
　　The shipping grows like **sedge.**

Here, weaving **the union of cities,**
　　With **hoar wakes** belting the **blue,**
From slip **to** slip, **past schooner** and ship,
　　The ferry's shuttles **flew : —**
Now, loosed from **its stall, on the yielding wall**
　　The steamboat paws and rears ;
The citizens pass **on** a pavement of glass,
　　And climb the frosted piers.

Where, in the November twilight,
    To the ribs of the skeleton bark
That stranded lay in the bend of the bay,
    Motionless, low, and dark,
Came ever three shags, like three lone hags,
    And sat o'er the troubled water,
Each nursing apart her shrivelled heart,
    With her mantle wrapped about her, —

Now over the ancient timbers
    Is built a magic deck;
Children run out with laughter and shout
    And dance around the wreck;
The fisherman near his long eel-spear
    Thrusts in through the ice, or stands
With fingers on lips, and now and then whips
    His sides with mittened hands.

II.

Alone and pensive I wander
    Far out from the city-wharf
To the buoy below in its cap of snow,
    Low stooping like a dwarf;

In the fading ray of the dull, brief day
    I wander and muse apart, —
For this frozen sea is a symbol to me
    Of many a human heart.

I think of the hopes deep sunken
    Like anchors under the ice, —
Of souls that wait for Love's sweet freight
    And the spices of Paradise :
Far off their barks are tossing
    On the billows of unrest,
And enter not in, for the hardness and sin
    That close the secret breast.

I linger, until, at evening,
    The town-roofs, towering high,
Uprear in the dimness their tall, dark chimneys,
    Indenting the sunset sky,
And the pendent spear on the edge of the pier
    Signals my homeward way,
As it gleams through the dusk like a walrus's tusk
    On the floes of a polar bay.

Then I think of the desolate households
    On which the day shuts down, —
What misery hides in the darkened tides
    Of life in yonder town!
I think of the lonely poet
    In his hours of coldness and pain,
His fancies full-freighted, like coasters belated,
    All frozen within his brain.

And I hearken to the moanings
    That come from the burdened bay:
As a camel, that kneels for his lading, reels,
    And cannot bear it away,
The mighty load is slowly
    Upheaved with struggle and pain
From centre to side, then the groaning tide
    Sinks heavily down again.

So day and night you may hear it
    Panting beneath its pack,
Till sailor and saw, till south-wind and thaw,
    Unbind it from its back.

O Sun! will thy beam ever gladden the stream
     And bid its burden depart?
O Life! all in vain do we strive with the chain
     That fetters and chills the heart?

Already in vision prophetic
     On yonder height I stand:
The gulls are gay upon the bay,
     The swallows on the land; —
'T is spring-time now; like an aspen-bough
     Shaken across the sky,
In the silvery light with twinkling flight
     The rustling plovers fly.

Aloft in the sunlit cordage
     Behold the climbing tar,
With his shadow beside on the sail white and wide,
     Climbing a shadow-spar!
Up the glassy stream with issuing steam
     The cutter crawls again,
All winged with cloud and buzzing loud
     Like a bee upon the pane.

The brigantine is bringing
    Her cargo to the quay,
The sloop flits by like a butterfly,
    The schooner skims the sea.
O young heart's trust, beneath the crust
    Of a chilling world congealed!
O love, whose flow the winter of woe
    With its icy hand hath sealed!

Learn patience from the lesson!
    Though the night be drear and long,
To the darkest sorrow there comes a morrow,
    A right to every wrong.
And as, when, having run his low course, the red Sun
    Comes charging gayly up here,
The white shield of Winter shall shiver and splinter
    At the touch of his golden spear, —

Then rushing under the bridges,
    And crushing among the piles,
In gray mottled masses the drift-ice passes,
    Like seaward-floating isles; —

So Life shall return from its solstice, **and burn**
    In trappings of gold and blue,
The world shall pass like **a shattered glass,**
    And the heaven of Love shine through.

OUR LADY.

OUR lady lives on the hillside here,
   Amid shady avenues, terraced lawns,
And fountains that leap like snow-white deer,
   With flashing antlers, and silver fawns;
And the twinkling wheels of the rich and great
Hum in and out of the high-arched gate;
And willing worshippers throng and wait,
   Where she wearily sits and yawns.

I remember her pretty and poor, —
   Now she has servants, jewels, and land:
She gave her heart to a poet-wooer, —
   To a wealthy suitor she bartered her hand.
A very desirable mate to choose, —
Believing in viands, in good port-juice,
In solid comfort and solid use, —
   Things simple to understand.

B

She loves **poetry,** music, and **art,** —
    He dines, and **races,** and smokes, **and shoots;**
She walks in an ideal realm apart, —
    He treads firm ground, in **his prosperous boots:**
A wise design; for you see, **'t is clear,**
Their paths do not lie **so unsuitably near**
As that ever either should **interfere**
    With the other's chosen **pursuits.**

By night, **as you roam through the rich** saloons,
    When music's purple **and crimson tones**
Float, in invisibly fine festoons,
    O'er the buzz **and** hum **of these human drones,**
You are ready **to swear that no happier pair**
Have lived than **your latter-day Adam there,**
And our sweet, pale Eve, **of the dark-furrowed hair,**
    Thick sown with glittering **stones.**

But **I** see, in the midst **of the music and talk,**
    A shape steal forth from the **glowing room,**
And pass, by a lonely cypress walk,
    Far down through **the** ghostly midnight gloom,

Sighing and sorrowful, wringing its hands,
And bruising its feet on the pointed sands,
Till, white, despairing, and dumb it stands,
    In the shadowy damp of a tomb.

The husband sprawls in his easy-chair,
    And smirks, and smacks, and tells his jest,
And strokes his chin with a satisfied air,
    And hooks his thumbs in his filagreed vest;
And the laugh rings round, and still she seems
To sit smiling there, and nobody deems
That her soul has gone down to that region of dreams,
    A weary, disconsolate guest.

Dim ghosts of happiness haunt the grot,
    Phantoms of buried hopes untold,
And ashen memories strew the spot
    Where her young heart's love lies coffined and cold.
With her burden of sin she kneeleth within,
And kisses, and presses, with fingers thin,
Brow, mouth, and bosom, and beautiful chin
    Of the dead that groweth not old.

He is ever there, with his dark wavy **hair,**
   Unchanged through years **of** anguish **and tears;**
His hands are pressed on his passionate **breast,**
   His eyes still plead with foreboding **and fears.**
O, she dwells not at all **in that stately hall!**
But, day **and** night, 'neath **the** cypresses **tall,**
She opens the coffin, uplifteth **the pall,**
   And the living **dead appears!**

THE MILL-POND.

THE linden, maple, and birch-tree bless,
   With cooling shades, the banks I press
In the midsummer sultriness;
And under the thickest shade of all
Singeth a musical waterfall.

The burnished breast of a silver pond
In the sunlight lieth beyond, —
Clear, and calm, and still as death,
Save where the south-wind's blurring breath,
Like an angel's pinion, fluttereth.

The south-wind moveth, but maketh no noise,
Nor ever disturbeth the delicate poise
Of the little fishing floats the boys
Sit idly watching on log and ledge:
It toucheth but softly the languid sedge,
Drooping all day by the water's edge.

In the thickets shady and cool
The white sheep tear their tender wool;
Pensively, one snowy lamb
Stands sighing beside the grassy dam;
Shaking and clashing the heavy boughs,
The limber colts and the sober cows
Down from the woody hillside come,
To stand in the shallows, and hark to the hum
Of the waterfall beating its airy drum.

Deep in the shadowy dell at noon
I lie, and list to the drowsy tune,
Fanned by the sweet south-wind;
And I think how like to the poet's mind
Are the skyey depths of the silver pond,
That in the sunlight lieth beyond
These lindens tall, and the slimy wall
Over which poureth the waterfall.

When the angry March winds blow,
And rains descend, and freshets flow
In torrent and rill from mountain and hill,

And the ponderous wheels of the sunken mill
Go round and round, with a sullen sound,
Rumbling, mumbling, half under ground, —
Hoarsely the waterfall singeth all day,
And the waters are streaked with marl and clay

But when these shaded banks I press,
In the midsummer sultriness,
Standeth all still the mumbling mill;
The quiet pond doth seem to thrill
With joys which all its windings fill;
And in its depths the eye may view
A world of soft and dreamy hue, —
Banks, and trees, and a sky of blue.

Willow and sedge, by the water's edge,
And children fishing from log and ledge;
The kingly oak with its myriad leaves, —
Even the web the spider weaves;
Lilies, cresses, and wild swamp grasses,
And every butterfly that passes,
The lakelet's placid bosom glasses.

THE RESTORED PICTURE.

IN later years, veiling its unblest face
    In a most loathsome place,
The cheap adornment of a house of shame,
    It hung, till, gnawed away
    By tooth of slow decay,
It fell, and parted from its mouldering frame.

The rotted canvas, faintly smiling still,
    From worldly puff and frill,
Its ghastly smile of coquetry and pride,
    Crumpling its faded charms
    And yellow jewelled arms,
Mere rubbish now, was rudely cast aside.

The shadow of a Genius crossed the gate:
    He, skilled to re-create
In old and ruined paintings their lost soul

And beauty, — one who knew
    The Master's touch by true,
Swift instinct, as the needle knows the pole, —

Looked on it, and straightway his searching eyes
    Saw through its coarse disguise
Of vulgar paint and grime and varnish stain
    The Art that slept beneath, —
    A chrysalis in its sheath,
That waited to be waked to life again.

Upon enduring canvas to renew
    Each wondrous trait and hue, —
This is the miracle, his chosen task!
    He bears it to his house,
    And there from lips and brows
With loving touch removes their alien mask.

For so on its perfection time had laid
    An early mellowing shade ;
Then hands unskilled, each seeking to impart

2

Fresh tints to form and face,
With some more modern grace,
Had buried quite the mighty Master's Art.

First, razed from the divine original,
Brow, cheek, and lid, went all
That outer shape of worldliness; when, lo!
Beneath the varnished crust
Of long imbedded dust
A fairer face appears, emerging slow, —

The features of a simple shepherdess!
Pure eyes, and golden tress,
And, lastly, crook in hand. But deeper still
The Master's work lies hid;
And still through lip and lid
Works the Restorer with unsparing skill.

Behold at length, in tender light revealed,
The soul so long concealed!
All heavenly faint at first, then softly bright,

As smiles the young-eyed Dawn
When darkness is withdrawn,
A shining angel breaks upon the sight!

Restored, perfected, after the divine
Imperishable design,
Lo now! that once despised and outcast thing
Holds its true place among
The fairest pictures hung
In the high palace of our Lord the King!

MY BROTHER BEN.

FROM the door where I stand I can see his fair land
    Sloping up to a broad sunny height;
The meadows new-shorn, and the green wavy corn,
  The buckwheat all blossoming white:
There a gay garden blooms, there are cedars like
    plumes,
And a rill from the mountain leaps up in a fountain,
  And shakes its glad locks in the light.

He dwells in the hall where the long shadows fall
  On the checkered and cool esplanade;
I live in a cottage secluded and small,
  By a gnarly old apple-tree's shade:
Side by side in the glen, I and my brother Ben,—
Just the river between us, with borders as green as
  The banks where in childhood we played.

But now nevermore upon river or shore
  He runs or he rows by my side;
For I am still poor, like our father before,
  And he, full of riches and pride,
Leads a life of such show, there is no room, you know,
In the very fine carriage he gained by his marriage
  For an old-fashioned brother to ride.

His wife, with her gold, gives him friends, I am told,
  With whom she is rather too gay, —
The senator's son, who is ready to run
  For her gloves and her fan, night or day,
And to gallop beside, when she wishes to ride:
O, no doubt 't is an honor to see smile upon her
  Such world-famous fellows as they!

Ah, brother of mine, while you sport, while you dine,
  While you drink of your wine like a lord,
You might curse, one would say, and grow jaundiced
    and gray,
  With such guests every day at your board!
But you sleek down your rage like a pard in its cage,

And blink in meek fashion through the bars of your
    passion,
  As husbands like you can afford.

For still you must think, as you eat, as you drink,
  As you hunt with your dogs and your guns,
How your pleasures are bought with the wealth that
      she brought,
  And you were once hunted by duns.
O, I envy you not your more fortunate lot:
I 've a wife all my own in my own little cot,
And with happiness, which is far better than riches,
  The cup of our love overruns.

We have bright, rosy girls, fair as ever an earl's,
  And the wealth of their curls is our gold;
O, their lisp and their laugh, they are sweeter by half
  Than the wine that you quaff red and old!
We have love-lighted looks, we have work, we have
    books,
  Our boys have grown manly and bold,

And they never shall blush, when their proud cousins
    brush
From the walls of their college such cobwebs of
    knowledge
  As careless young fingers may hold.

Keep your pride and your cheer, for we need them
    not here,
  And for me far too dear they would prove;
For gold is but gloss, and possessions are dross,
  And gain is all loss, without love.
Yon severing tide is not fordless or wide, —
The soul's blue abysses our households divide:
Down through the still river they deepen forever,
  Like the skies it reflects from above.

Still my brother thou art, though our lives lie apart,
  Path from path, heart from heart, more and more.
O, I have not forgot, — O, remember you not
  Our room in the cot by the shore?

And a night soon will come, when the murmur and
    hum

  Of our days shall be dumb evermore,

And again we shall lie side by side, you and I,

Beneath the green cover you helped to lay over

  Our honest old father of yore.

THE PEWEE.

THE listening Dryads hushed the woods;
 The boughs were thick, and thin and few
 The golden ribbons fluttering through;
Their sun-embroidered, leafy hoods
 The lindens lifted to the blue:
Only a little forest-brook
The farthest hem of silence shook:
When in the hollow shades I heard, —
Was it a spirit, or a bird?
Or, strayed from Eden, desolate,
Some Peri calling to her mate,
 Whom nevermore her mate would cheer?
  " Pe-ri! pe-ri! peer!"

Through rocky clefts the brooklet fell
 'With plashy pour, that scarce was sound,
 But only quiet less profound,

A stillness fresh and audible:
  A yellow leaflet to the ground
Whirled noiselessly: with wing of gloss
A hovering sunbeam brushed the moss,
And, wavering brightly over it,
Sat like a butterfly alit:
The owlet in his open door
Stared roundly: while the breezes bore
  The plaint to far-off places drear, —
    " Pe-ree! pe-ree! peer!"

To trace it in its green retreat
  I sought among the boughs in vain;
  And followed still the wandering strain,
So melancholy and so sweet
  The dim-eyed violets yearned with pain.
'T was now a sorrow in the air,
Some nymph's immortalized despair
Haunting the woods and waterfalls;
And now, at long, sad intervals,
Sitting unseen in dusky shade,
His plaintive pipe some fairy played,

With long-drawn cadence thin and clear, —
    "Pe-wee! pe-wee! peer!"

Long-drawn and clear its closes were, —
  As if the hand of Music through
  The sombre robe of Silence drew
A thread of golden gossamer:
  So pure a flute the fairy blew.
Like beggared princes of the wood,
In silver rags the birches stood;
The hemlocks, lordly counsellors,
Were dumb; the sturdy servitors,
In beechen jackets patched and gray,
Seemed waiting spellbound all the day
  That low, entrancing note to hear, —
    "Pe-wee! pe-wee! peer!"

I quit the search, and sat me down
  Beside the brook, irresolute,
  And watched a little bird in suit
Of sober olive, soft and brown,
  Perched in the maple-branches, mute:

With greenish gold its vest **was fringed,**
Its tiny **cap** was ebon-tinged,
With ivory pale **its wings** were **barred,**
And its dark eyes were tender-starred.
"Dear bird," I said, "what is thy name?"
And thrice the mournful answer **came,**
  So faint and far, and yet so **near,** —
    "Pe-wee! pe-wee! peer!"

For so I found **my forest bird,** —
  The pewee of the loneliest **woods,**
  Sole singer in these solitudes,
Which never robin's whistle stirred,
  Where never bluebird's **plume intrudes.**
Quick darting through **the dewy morn,**
The **redstart** trilled **his twittering horn,**
And vanished in **thick boughs: at even,**
Like liquid pearls fresh **showered from heaven,**
The high notes of the lone wood-thrush
Fall **on** the forest's holy hush:
  But thou all day complainest **here,** —
    "Pe-wee! pe-wee! **peer!"**

Hast thou, too, in thy little breast,
   Strange longings for a happier lot, —
   For love, for life, thou know'st not what, —
A yearning, and a vague unrest,
   For something still which thou hast not? —
Thou soul of some benighted child
That perished, crying in the wild!
Or lost, forlorn, and wandering maid,
By love allured, by love betrayed,
Whose spirit with her latest sigh
Arose, a little wingéd cry,
   Above her chill and mossy bier!
      "Dear me! dear me! dear!"

Ah, no such piercing sorrow mars
   The pewee's life of cheerful ease!
   He sings, or leaves his song to seize
An insect sporting in the bars
   Of mild bright light that gild the trees.
A very poet he! For him
All pleasant places still and dim:
His heart, a spark of heavenly fire,

Burns with undying, sweet desire :

And so he sings ; and so his song,

Though heard not by the **hurrying throng,**

    Is solace **to** the pensive ear :

      " Pewee ! pewee ! peer !"

BEYOND.

FROM her own fair dominions,
    Long since, with shorn pinions,
    My spirit was banished:
But around her still hover, in vigils and dreams,
Ethereal visitants, voices, and gleams,
    That forever remind her
    Of something behind her
        Long vanished.

    Through the listening night,
    With mysterious flight,
        Pass those winged intimations:
Like stars shot from heaven, their still voices fall to me;
Far and departing, they signal and call to me,
    Strangely beseeching me,
    Chiding, yet teaching me
        Patience

Then at times, oh! at times,
To their luminous climes
I pursue as a swallow!
To the river of Peace, and its solacing shades,
To the haunts of my lost ones, in heavenly glades,
With strong aspirations
Their pinions' vibrations
I follow.

O heart, be thou patient!
Though here I am stationed
A season in durance,
The chain of the world I will cheerfully wear;
For, spanning my soul like a rainbow, I bear,
With the yoke of my lowly
Condition, a holy
Assurance, —

That never in vain
Does the spirit maintain
Her eternal allegiance:
Through suffering and yearning, like Infancy learning

Its lesson, we linger; then, skyward returning,
    On plumes fully grown
    We depart to our own
        Native regions!

MIDWINTER.

THE speckled sky is dim with snow,
The light flakes falter and fall slow;
Athwart the hill-top, rapt and pale,
Silently drops a silvery veil;
And all the valley is shut in
By flickering curtains gray and thin.

But cheerily the chickadee
Singeth to me on fence and tree;
The snow sails round him, as he sings,
White as the down of angels' wings.

I watch the slow flakes as they fall
On bank and brier and broken wall;
Over the orchard, waste and brown,
All noiselessly they settle down,
Tipping the apple-boughs, and each
Light quivering twig of plum and peach.

On turf and curb and bower-roof
The snow-storm spreads its ivory woof;
It paves with pearl the garden-walk;
And lovingly round tattered stalk
And shivering stem its magic weaves
A mantle fair as lily-leaves.

The hooded beehive, small and low,
Stands like a maiden in the snow;
And the old door-slab is half hid
Under an alabaster lid.

All day it snows: the sheeted post
Gleams in the dimness like a ghost;
All day the blasted oak has stood
A muffled wizard of the wood;
Garland and airy cap adorn
The sumach and the wayside thorn,
And clustering spangles lodge and shine
In the dark tresses of the pine.

The ragged bramble, dwarfed and old,
Shrinks like a beggar in the cold ;
In surplice white the cedar stands,
And blesses him with priestly hands.

Still cheerily the chickadee
Singeth to me on fence and tree :
But in my inmost ear is heard
The music of a holier bird ;
And heavenly thoughts, as soft and white
As snow-flakes, on my soul alight,
Clothing with love my lonely heart,
Healing with peace each bruiséd part,
Till all my being seems to be
Transfigured by their purity.

MIDSUMMER.

AROUND this lovely valley rise
The purple hills of Paradise.

O softly on yon banks of haze
Her rosy face the Summer lays!

Becalmed along the azure sky,
The argosies of cloudland lie,
Whose shores, with many a shining rift,
Far off their pearl-white peaks uplift.

Through all the long midsummer-day
The meadow-sides are sweet with hay.
I seek the coolest sheltered seat,
Just where the field and forest meet, —
Where grow the pine-trees tall and bland,
The ancient oaks austere and grand,

And fringy roots and pebbles fret
The ripples of the rivulet.

I watch the mowers, as they go
Through the tall grass, a white-sleeved row.
With even stroke their scythes they swing,
In tune their merry whetstones ring.
Behind the nimble youngsters run,
And toss the thick swaths in the sun.
The cattle graze, while, warm and still,
Slopes the broad pasture, basks the hill,
And bright, where summer breezes break,
The green wheat crinkles like a lake.

The butterfly and humble-bee
Come to the pleasant woods with me;
Quickly before me runs the quail,
Her chickens skulk behind the rail;
High up the lone wood-pigeon sits,
And the woodpecker pecks and flits.
Sweet woodland music sinks and swells,
The brooklet rings its tinkling bells,

The swarming insects drone and hum,
The partridge beats his throbbing drum.
The squirrel leaps among the boughs,
And chatters in his leafy house.
The oriole flashes by; and, look!
Into the mirror of the brook,
Where the vain bluebird trims his coat,
Two tiny feathers fall and float.

As silently, as tenderly,
The down of peace descends on me.
O, this is peace! I have no need
Of friend to talk, of book to read:
A dear Companion here abides;
Close to my thrilling heart He hides;
The holy silence is His Voice:
I lie and listen, and rejoice.

MY COMRADE AND I.

WE two have grown up so divinely together,
 Flower within flower from seed within seed,
The sagest astrologer cannot say whether
 His being or mine was first called and decreed.
In the life before birth, by inscrutable ties,
 We were linked each to each; I am bound up in him;
He sickens, I languish; without me he dies;
 I am life of his life, he is limb of my limb.

Twin babes from one cradle, I tottered about with him,
 Chased the bright butterflies, singing, a boy with him;
Still as a man I am borne in and out with him,
 Sup with him, sleep with him, suffer, enjoy with him.
Faithful companion, me long he has carried
 Unseen in his bosom, a lamp to his feet;
More near than a bridegroom, to him I am married,
 As light in the sunbeam is wedded to heat.

If my beam be withdrawn he is senseless and blind;
   I am sight to his vision, I hear with his ears;
His the marvellous brain, I the masterful mind;
   I laugh with his laughter and weep with his tears
So well that the ignorant deem us but one:
   They see but one shape and they name us one name.
O pliant accomplice! what deeds we have done,
   Thus banded together for glory or shame!

When evil waylays us, and passion surprises,
   And we are too feeble to strive or to fly,
When hunger compels or when pleasure entices,
   Which most is the sinner, my comrade or I?
And when over perils and pains and temptations
   I triumph, where still I should falter and faint,
But for him, iron-nerved for heroical patience,
   Whose then is the virtue, and which is the saint?

Am I the one sinner? of honors sole claimant
   For actions which only we two can perform?
Am I the true creature, and thou but the raiment?
   Thou magical mantle, all vital and warm,

3	D

Wrapped about me, a screen from **the rough winds of**
    Time,
  Of texture so flexile to feature and gesture!
Can ever I part from thee? Is **there a clime**
  Where Life needeth **not this** terrestrial **vesture?**

When comes the **sad** summons **to sever the sweet**
  Subtle tie that unites us, and tremulous, fearful,
I feel thy **loosed fetters** depart **from** my feet;
  When friends gathered **round us,** pale-visaged and
    tearful,
Beweep and bewail thee, thou fair earthly **prison!**
  And kiss thy cold doors, for thy **inmate mis-**
    taken;
Their eyes seeing not the **freed captive, arisen**
  From thy trammels **unclasped and thy shackles**
    downshaken;

O, then shall I linger, **reluctant to break**
  The dear sensitive chains that about me have grown?
And all this bright world, can I bear **to forsake**
  Its embosoming **beauty** and love, and **alone**

Journey on to I know not what regions untried?
   Exists there, beyond the dim cloud-rack of death,
Such life as enchants us? O skies arched and wide!
   O delicate senses! O exquisite breath!

Ah, tenderly, tenderly over thee hovering,
   I shall look down on thee empty and cloven,
Pale mould of my being!—thou visible covering
   Wherefrom my invisible raiment is woven.
Though sad be the passage, nor pain shall appall me,
   Nor parting, assured, wheresoever I range
The glad fields of existence, that naught can befall me
   That is not still beautiful, blessed, and strange.

THE WOLVES.

YE who listen to stories told,
 When hearths are cheery and nights are cold,

Of the lone wood-side, and the hungry pack
That howls on the fainting traveller's track, —

Flame-red eyeballs that waylay,
By the wintry moon, the belated sleigh, —

The lost child sought in the dismal wood,
The little shoes and the stains of blood

On the trampled snow, — O ye that hear,
With thrills of pity, or chills of fear,

Wishing some angel had been sent
To shield the hapless and innocent, —

Know ye the fiend that is crueller far
Than the gaunt gray herds of the forest are?

Swiftly vanish the wild fleet tracks
Before the rifle and woodman's axe:

But hark to the coming of unseen feet,
Pattering by night through the city street!

Each wolf that dies in the woodland brown
Lives a spectre and haunts the town.

By square and market they slink and prowl,
In lane and alley they leap and howl.

All night they snuff and snarl before
The poor patched window and broken door.

They paw the clapboards and claw the latch,
At every crevice they whine and scratch.

Their tongues are subtle and long and thin,
And they lap the living blood within.

Icy keen are the **teeth** that tear,
Red as ruin the eyes that **glare.**

Children crouched in corners cold
Shiver in tattered garments **old,**

And **start** from sleep **with bitter pangs**
At the touch **of the** phantoms' viewless fangs.

Weary the mother **and worn with** strife,
Still she watches and fights **for life.**

But her hand is feeble, and weapon small:
One little **needle against them all !**

In evil hour the daughter **fled**
From her poor shelter **and wretched** bed.

Through **the** city's pitiless solitude
To the door **of sin** the wolves pursued.

Fierce the father and grim with **want,**
His heart is gnawed by the spectres gaunt.

Frenzied stealing forth by night,
With whetted knife to the desperate fight,

He thought to smite the spectres dead,
But he smites his brother man instead.

O you that listen to stories told,
When hearths are cheery and nights are cold,

Weep no more at the tales you hear,
The danger is close, and the wolves are near.

Shudder not at the murderer's name,
Marvel not at the maiden's shame.

Pass not by with averted eye
The door where the stricken children cry.

But when the beat of the phantom feet
Sounds by night through the stormy street,

Follow thou where the spectres glide;
Stand like Hope by the mother's side;

And be thyself the angel sent
To shield the hapless **and innocent.**

He giveth little **who gives but tears,**
He giveth his best **who aids and cheers.**

He does well in **the forest wild**
Who slays **the monster and saves the child;**

But he does better, and **merits more,**
Who drives the **wolf from the poor man's door.**

LA CANTATRICE.

BY day, at a high oak desk I stand,
   And trace in a ledger line by line;
But at five o'clock yon dial's hand
  Opens the cage wherein I pine;
And as faintly the stroke from the belfry peals
Down through the thunder of hoofs and wheels,
I wonder if ever a monarch feels
    Such royal joy as mine!

Beatrice is dressed, and her carriage waits;
   I know she has heard that signal-chime;
And my strong heart leaps and palpitates,
  As lightly the winding stair I climb
To her fragrant room, where the winter's gloom
Is changed by the heliotrope's perfume,
And the curtained sunset's crimson bloom,
    To love's own summer prime.

3*

She meets me there, so strangely fair
    That my soul aches with a happy pain; —
A pressure, a touch of her true lips, such
    As a seraph might give and take again;
A hurried whisper, "Adieu! adieu!
They wait for me while I stay for you!"
And a parting smile of her blue eyes through
    The glimmering carriage-pane.

Then thoughts of the past come crowding fast
    On a blissful track of love and sighs; —
O, well I toiled, and these poor hands soiled,
    That her song might bloom in Italian skies! —
The pains and fears of those lonely years,
The nights of longing and hope and tears, —
Her heart's sweet debt, and the long arrears
    Of love in those faithful eyes!

O night! be friendly to her and me! —
    To box and pit and gallery swarm
The expectant throngs; — I am there to see; —
    And now she is bending her radiant form

To the clapping crowd;—I am thrilled and proud;
My dim eyes look through a misty cloud,
And my joy mounts up on the plaudits loud,
    Like a sea-bird on a storm!

She has waved her hand; the tumultuous rush
  Of applause sinks down; and silverly
Her voice glides forth on the quivering hush,
  Like the white-robed moon on a tremulous sea!
And wherever her shining influence calls,
I swing on the billow that swells and falls,—
I know no more,—till the very walls
    Seem shouting with jubilee!

O, little she cares for the fop who airs
  His glove and glass, or the gay array
Of fans and perfumes, of jewels and plumes,
  Where wealth and pleasure have met to pay
Their nightly homage to her sweet song;
But over the bravas clear and strong,
Over all the flaunting and fluttering throng,
    She smiles my soul away!

Why am I happy? why am I proud?

   O, can it be true she is all my own? —

I make my way through the ignorant crowd;

   I know, I know where my love hath flown.

Again we meet; I am here at her feet,

And with kindling kisses and promises sweet,

Her glowing, victorious lips repeat

   That they sing for me alone!

BEAUTY.

FOND lover of the Ideal Fair,
  My soul, eluded everywhere,
Is lapsed into a sweet despair.

Perpetual pilgrim, seeking ever,
Baffled, enamored, finding never;
Each morn the cheerful chase renewing,
Misled, bewildered, still pursuing;
Not all my lavished years have bought
One steadfast smile from her I sought,
But sidelong glances, glimpsing light,
A something far too fine for sight,
Veiled voices, far-off thridding strains,
And precious agonies and pains:
Not love, but only love's dear wound
And exquisite unrest I found.

At early morn I saw her pass
The lone lake's blurred and quivering glass;
Her trailing veil of amber mist
The unbending beaded clover kissed;
And straight I hasted to waylay
Her coming by the willowy way; —
But, swift companion of the Dawn,
She left her footprints on the lawn,
And, in arriving, she was gone.

Alert I ranged the winding shore;
Her luminous presence flashed before;
The wild-rose and the daisies wet
From her light touch were trembling yet;
Faint smiled the conscious violet;
Each bush and brier and rock betrayed
Some tender sign her parting made;
And when far on her flight I tracked
To where the thunderous cataract
O'er walls of foamy ledges broke,
She vanished in the vapory smoke.

To-night I pace this pallid **floor,**
The sparkling waves curl up the shore,
The August moon is flushed and full ;
The soft, low winds, the liquid lull,
The whited, silent, misty realm,
The wan-blue heaven, **each ghostly elm,**
All these, her ministers, conspire
To fill my bosom with the fire
And sweet delirium of desire.
Enchantress ! leave thy sheeny height,
Descend, be all mine own this night,
Transfuse, enfold, entrance me quite !
Or break thy spell, my **heart restore,**
And **disenchant** me evermore !

SERVICE.

WHEN I beheld a lover woo
    A maid unwilling,
And saw what lavish deeds men do,
  Hope's flagon filling, —
What vines are tilled, what wines are spilled,
  And madly wasted,
To fill the flask that 's never filled,
  And rarely tasted:

Devouring all life's heritage,
  And inly starving;
Dulling the spirit's mystic edge,
  The banquet carving;
Feasting with Pride, that Barmecide
  Of unreal dishes;
And wandering ever in a wide,
  Wide world of wishes:

For gain **or** glory lands and seas
   Endlessly ranging,
Safety **and** years and health and ease
   Freely exchanging : —
When, **ever** as **I moved, I saw**
   The world's contagion,
Then turned, O Love! to **thy sweet law**
   And compensation, —

Well might red shame my cheek consume!
   O service slighted!
O Bride **of** Paradise, to whom
   I long was plighted!
Do I with burning **lips profess**
   To serve thee wholly,
Yet labor less for blessedness
   Than fools for folly?

The wary worldling spread his toils
   Whilst I was sleeping;
The wakeful miser locked his spoils,
   Keen vigils keeping :

I loosed the latches of my soul
　To pleading Pleasure,
Who stayed one little hour, and stole
　My heavenly treasure.

A friend for friend's sake will endure
　Sharp provocations;
And knaves are cunning to secure,
　By cringing patience,
And smiles upon a smarting cheek,
　Some dear advantage, —
Swathing their grievances in meek
　Submission's bandage.

Yet for thy sake I will not take
　One drop of trial,
But raise rebellious hands to break
　The bitter vial.
At hardship's surly-visaged churl
　My spirit sallies;
And melts, O Peace! thy priceless pearl
　In passion's chalice.

Yet never quite, in darkest night,
  Was I forsaken :
Down trickles still some starry rill
  My heart to waken.
O Love Divine ! could I resign
  This changeful spirit
To walk thy ways, what wealth of grace
  Might I inherit !

If one poor flower of thanks to thee
  Be truly given,
All night thou snowest down to me
  Lilies of heaven !
One task of human love fulfilled,
  Thy glimpses tender
My days of lonely labor gild
  With gleams of splendor !

One prayer, — " Thy will, not mine ! " — and bright,
  O'er all my being,
Breaks blissful light, that gives to sight
  A subtler seeing ;

Straightway mine ear is tuned to hear
  Ethereal numbers,
Whose secret symphonies insphere
  The dull earth's slumbers.

"Thy will!" — and I am armed to meet
  Misfortune's volleys;
For every sorrow I have sweet,
  O, sweetest solace!
"Thy will!" — no more I hunger sore,
  For angels feed me;
Henceforth for days, by peaceful ways,
  They gently lead me.

For me the diamond dawns are set
  In rings of beauty,
And all my paths are dewy wet
  With pleasant duty;
Beneath the boughs of calm content
  My hammock swinging,
In their green tent my eves are spent,
  Thy praises singing.

AT SEA.

THE night is made for cooling shade,
   For silence, and for sleep;
And when I was a child, I laid
My hands upon my breast and prayed,
   And sank to slumbers deep:
Childlike as then, I lie to-night,
And watch my lonely cabin light.

Each movement of the swaying lamp
   Shows how the vessel reels:
As o'er her deck the billows tramp,
And all her timbers strain and cramp,
   With every shock she feels,
It starts and shudders, while it burns,
And in its hingéd socket turns.

Now swinging slow, and slanting low,
   It almost level lies;

And yet I know, while to and fro
I watch the seeming pendule go
  With restless fall and rise,
The steady shaft is still upright,
Poising its little globe of light.

O hand of God! O lamp of peace!
  O promise of my soul! —
Though weak, and tossed, and ill at ease,
Amid the roar of smiting seas,
  The ship's convulsive roll,
I own, with love and tender awe,
Yon perfect type of faith and law!

A heavenly trust my spirit calms,
  My soul is filled with light:
The ocean sings his solemn psalms,
The wild winds chant: I cross my palms,
  Happy as if, to-night,
Under the cottage-roof, again
I heard the soothing summer-rain.

REAL ESTATE.

THE pleasant grounds are greenly turfed and graded;
    A sturdy porter waiteth at the gate;
The graceful avenues, serenely shaded,
And curving paths, are interlaced and braided
    In many a maze around my fair estate.

Here blooms the early hyacinth, and clover
    And amaranth and myrtle wreathe the ground;
The pensive lily leans her pale cheek over;
And hither comes the bee, light-hearted rover,
    Wooing the sweet-breathed flowers with soothing
      sound.

Intwining, in their manifold digressions,
    Lands of my neighbors, wind these peaceful ways.
The masters, coming to their calm possessions,
Followed in solemn state by long processions,
    Make quiet journeys these still summer days.

This is my freehold ! Elms and fringy larches,
　　Maples and pines, and stately firs of Norway,
Build round me their green pyramids and arches;
Sweetly the robin sings, while slowly marches
　　The stately pageant past my verdant doorway.

O, sweetly sing the robin and the sparrow !
　　But the pale tenant very silent rides.
A low green roof receiveth him ; — so narrow
His hollowed tenement, a school-boy's arrow
　　Might span the space betwixt its grassy sides.

The flowers around him ring their wind-swung chalices,
　　A great bell tolls the pageant's slow advance.
The poor alike, and lords of parks and palaces,
From all their busy schemes, their fears and fallacies,
　　Find here their rest and sure inheritance.

No more hath Cæsar or Sardanapalus !
　　Of all our wide dominions, soon or late,
Only a fathom's space can aught avail us ;
This is the heritage that shall not fail us :
　　Here man at last comes to his Real Estate.

"Secure to him and to his heirs forever"!
    Nor wealth nor want shall vex his spirit more.
Treasures of hope and love and high endeavor
Follow their blest proprietor ; but never
    Could pomp or riches pass this little door.

Flatterers attend him, but alone he enters, —
    Shakes off the dust of earth, no more to roam.
His trial ended, sealed his soul's indentures,
The wanderer, weary from his long adventures,
    Beholds the peace of his eternal home.

Lo, more than life Man's great Estate comprises!
    While for the earthly corner of his mansion
A little nook in shady Time suffices,
The rainbow-pillared heavenly roof arises
    Ethereal in limitless expansion !

4

THE MASKERS.

YESTERNIGHT, as late I strayed
   Through the orchard's mottled shade, —
Coming to the moonlit alleys,
Where the sweet south-wind, that dallies
All day with the Queen of Roses,
All night on her breast reposes, —
Drinking from the dewy blooms,
Silences, and scented glooms
Of the warm-breathed summer night,
Long, deep draughts of pure delight, —
Quick the shaken foliage parted,
And from out its shadows darted
Dwarf-like forms, with hideous faces,
Cries, contortions, and grimaces.

Still I stood beneath the lonely,
Sighing lilacs, saying only, —

"Little friends, you can't alarm me;
Well I know you would not harm me!"
Straightway dropped each painted mask,
Sword of lath, and paper casque,
And a troop of rosy girls
Ran and kissed me through their curls.

Caught within their net of graces,
I looked round on shining faces.
Sweetly through the moonlit alleys
Rang their laughter's silver sallies.
Then along the pathway, light .
With the white bloom of the night,
I went peaceful, pacing slow,
Captive held in arms of snow.

Happy maids! of you I learn
Heavenly maskers to discern!
So, when seeming griefs and harms
Fill life's garden with alarms,
Through its inner walks enchanted
I will ever move undaunted.

Love hath messengers **that borrow**
Tragic masks of fear and sorrow,
When **they come to** do us kindness, —
And but for our tears and blindness,
We should see, through **each disguise,**
Cherub cheeks and angel **eyes.**

BY THE RIVER.

I.

IN the beautiful greenwood's charméd light,
   And down through the meadows wide and bright,
Deep in the silence, and smooth in the gleam,
For ever and ever flows the stream.

Where the mandrakes grow, and the pale, thin grass
The airy scarf of the woodland weaves,
By dim, enchanted paths I pass,
Crushing the twigs and the last year's leaves.

Over the wave, by the crystal brink,
A kingfisher sits on a low, dead limb:
He is always sitting there, I think, —
And another, within the crystal brink,
Is always pendent under him.

I know where an old tree leans across
From bank to bank, an ancient tree,
Quaintly cushioned with curious moss,
A bridge for the cool wood-nymphs and me:
Half seen they flit, while here I sit
By the magical water, watching it.

In its bosom swims the fair phantasm
Of a subterraneous azure chasm,
So soft and clear, you would say the stream
Was dreaming of heaven a visible dream.

Where the noontide basks, and its warm rays tint
The nettles and clover and scented mint,
And the crinkled airs, that curl and quiver,
Drop their wreaths in the mirroring river, —
Under the shaggy magnificent drapery
Of many a wild-woven native grapery, —
By ivy-bowers, and banks of violets,
And golden hillocks, and emerald islets,
Along its sinuous shining bed.
In sheets of splendor it lies outspread.

In the twilight stillness and solitude
Of green caves roofed by the brooding wood,
Where the woodbine swings, and beneath the trailing
Sprays of the queenly elm-tree sailing, —
By ribbed and wave-worn ledges shimmering,
Gilding the rocks with a rippled glimmering,
All pictured over in shade and sun,
The wavering silken waters run.

Upon this mossy trunk I sit,
Over the river, watching it.
A shadowed face peers up at me;
And another tree in the chasm I see,
Clinging above the abyss it spans;
The broad boughs curve their spreading fans,
From side to side, in the nether air;
And phantom birds in the phantom branches
Mimic the birds above; and there,
Oh! far below, solemn and slow,
The white clouds roll the crumbling snow
Of ever-pendulous avalanches, ·
Till the brain grows giddy, gazing through
Their wild, wide rifts of bottomless blue.

II.

THROUGH the river, and through **the rifts**
Of the sundered earth I gaze,
While Thought on dreamy **pinion drifts,**
Over cerulean bays,
Into the deep ethereal sea
Of her **own** serene eternity.

Transfigured **by** my trancéd eye,
Wood and meadow, **and stream and sky,**
Like vistas of a vision lie :
THE WORLD is the River that flickers by.

.

Its skies are the blue-arched centuries ;
And its forms are the transient images
Flung on **thé** flowing film of Time
By the steadfast shores of a fadeless clime.

As yonder wave-side willows grow,
Substance above, and shadow below,

The golden slopes of that upper sphere
Hang their imperfect landscapes here.

Fast by the Tree of Life, which shoots
Duplicate forms from selfsame roots,
Under the fringes of Paradise,
The crystal brim of the River lies.

There are banks of Peace, whose lilies pure
Paint on the wave their portraiture;
And many a holy influence,
That climbs to God like the breath of prayer,
Creeps quivering into the glass of sense,
To bless the immortals mirrored there.

Through realms of Poesy, whose white cliffs
Cloud its deeps with their hieroglyphs,
Alpine fantasies heaped and wrought
At will by the frolicsome winds of Thought, —
By shores of Beauty, whose colors pass
Faintly into the misty glass, —
By hills of Truth, whose glories show

4

L

Distorted, broken, and dimmed, as we know, —
Kissed by the tremulous long green tress
Of the glistening tree of Happiness,
Which ever our aching grasp eludes
With sweet illusive similitudes, —
All pictured over in shade and gleam,
For ever and ever runs the Stream.

The orb that burns in the rifts of space
Is the adumbration of God's Face.
My Soul leans over the murmuring flow,
And I am the image it sees below.

THE NAME IN THE BARK.

THE self of so long ago,
  And the self I struggle to know,
I sometimes think we are two, — or are we shadows
  of one?
  To-day the shadow I am
  Returns in the sweet summer calm
To trace where the earlier shadow flitted awhile in the
  sun.

  Once more in the dewy morn
  I came through the whispering corn;
Cool to my fevered cheek soft breezy kisses were blown;
  The ribboned and tasselled grass
  Leaned over the flattering glass,
And the sunny waters trilled the same low musical tone.

  To the gray old birch I came,
  Where I whittled my school-boy name:

The nimble squirrel once more ran skippingly over the
      rail,
    The blackbirds down among
    The alders noisily sung,
And under the blackberry-brier whistled the serious quail.

    I came, remembering well
    How my little shadow fell,
As I painfully reached and wrote to leave to the
      future a sign :
    There, stooping a little, I found
    A half-healed, curious wound,
An ancient scar in the bark, but no initial of mine!

    Then the wise old boughs overhead
    Took counsel together, and said, —
And the buzz of their leafy lips like a murmur of
      prophecy passed, —
    "He is busily carving a name
    In the tough old wrinkles of fame ;
But, cut he as deep as he may, the lines will close
      over at last!"

Sadly I pondered awhile,

Then I lifted my soul with a smile,

And I said, " Not cheerful men, but anxious children
are we,

Still hurting ourselves with the knife,

As we toil at the letters of life,

Just marring a little the rind, never piercing the
heart of the tree."

And now by the rivulet's brink

I leisurely saunter, and think

How idle this strife will appear when circling ages
have run,

If then the real I am

Descend from the heavenly calm,

To trace where the shadow I seem once flitted awhile
in the sun.

LYRICS OF THE WAR.

THE LAST RALLY.

[NOVEMBER, 1864.]

RALLY! rally! rally!
  Arouse the slumbering land!
Rally! rally! from mountain and valley,
  From city and ocean-strand!
Ye sons of the West, America's best!
  New Hampshire's men of might!
From prairie and crag unfurl the flag,
  And rally to the fight!

Armies of untried heroes,
  Disguised in craftsman and clerk!
Ye men of the coast, invincible host!
  Come, every one, to the work, —
From the fisherman gray as the salt-sea spray
  That on Long Island breaks,

THE LAST RALLY.

To the youth who tills the uttermost hills
  By the blue northwestern lakes!

Old men shall fight with the ballot,
  Weapon the last and best, —
And the bayonet, with blood red-wet,
  Shall write the will of the rest;
And the boys shall fill men's places,
  And the little maid shall rock
Her doll as she sits with her grandam and knits
  An unknown hero's sock.

And the hearts of heroic mothers,
  And the deeds of noble wives,
With their power to bless shall aid no less
  Than the brave who give their lives.
The rich their gold shall bring, and the old
  Shall help us with their prayers;
While hovering hosts of pallid ghosts
  Attend us unawares.

From the ghastly fields of Shiloh
  Muster the phantom bands,

From Virginia's swamps, and Death's white camps
  On Carolina sands ;
From Fredericksburg, and Gettysburg,
  I see them gathering fast ;
And up from Manassas, what is it that passes
  Like thin clouds in the blast ?

From the Wilderness, where blanches
  The nameless skeleton ;
From Vicksburg's slaughter and red-streaked water,
  And the trenches of Donelson ;
From the cruel, cruel prisons,
  Where their bodies pined away,
From groaning decks, from sunken wrecks,
  They gather with us to-day.

And they say to us, "Rally ! rally !
  The work is almost done !
Ye harvesters, sally from mountain and valley
  And reap the fields we won !
We sowed for endless years of peace,
  We harrowed and watered well ;

Our dying deeds were the scattered seeds:
  Shall they perish where they fell?"

And their brothers, left behind them
  In the deadly roar and clash
Of cannon and sword, by fort and ford,
  And the carbine's quivering flash, —
Before the Rebel citadel
  Just trembling to its fall,
From Georgia's glens, from Florida's fens,
  For us they call, they call!

The life-blood of the tyrant
  Is ebbing fast away;
Victory waits at her opening gates,
  And smiles on our array;
With solemn eyes the Centuries
  Before us watching stand,
And Love lets down his starry crown
  To bless the future land.

One more sublime endeavor
  And behold the dawn of Peace!

One more endeavor, and war forever
　Throughout the land shall cease !
For ever and ever the vanquished power
　Of Slavery shall be slain,
And Freedom's stained and trampled flower
　Shall blossom white again !

THE COLOR-BEARER.

'T WAS a fortress to be stormed:
  Boldly right in view they formed,
All as quiet as a regiment parading:
  Then in front a line of flame!
  Then at left and right the same!
Two platoons received a furious enfilading.
    To their places still they filed,
    And they smiled at the wild
        Cannonading.

"'T will be over in an hour!
'T will not be much of a shower!
Never mind, my boys," said he, "a little drizzling!"
    Then to cross that fatal plain,
    Through the whirring, hurtling rain
Of the grape-shot, and the minie-bullets' whistling!
    But he nothing heeds nor shuns,
    As he runs with the guns
        Brightly bristling!

Leaving trails of dead and dying
In their track, yet forward flying
Like a breaker where the gale of conflict rolled them,
With a foam of flashing light
Borne before them on their bright
Burnished barrels, — O, 't was fearful to behold them!
While from ramparts roaring loud
Swept a cloud like a shroud
To enfold them!

O, his color was the first!
Through the burying cloud he burst,
With the standard to the battle forward slanted!
Through the belching, blinding breath
Of the flaming jaws of Death,
With the banner on the bastion to be planted!
By the screaming shot that fell,
And the yell of the shell,
Nothing daunted.

Right against the bulwark dashing,
Over tangled branches crashing,

'Mid the plunging volleys thundering **ever louder,**
　　There **the** clambers, **there he stands,**
　　With the ensign in his hands, —
O, was ever hero handsomer or prouder?
　　Streaked with battle-sweat and slime
　　And sublime in **the grime**
　　　Of the powder!

　　'T was six minutes, at the least,
　　Ere the closing combat ceased, —
Near as we the mighty moments then could measure, —
　　And we held our souls with awe,
　　Till his haughty flag we saw
On the lifting vapors drifting o'er the embrasure,
　　Saw it glimmer in our tears,
　　While our ears heard the cheers
　　　Rend the azure!

　　Through the abatis they **broke,**
　　Through the surging cannon-smoke,
And they drove the foe **before like frightened cattle.**

O, but never wound was his,
For in other wars than this,
Where the volleys of Life's conflict roll and rattle,
He must still, as he was wont,
In the front bear the brunt
Of the battle.

He shall guide the van of Truth,
And in manhood, as in youth,
Be her fearless, be her peerless Color-Bearer!
With his high and bright example,
Like a banner brave and ample,
Ever leading through receding clouds of Error,
To the empire of the Strong,
And to Wrong he shall long
Be a terror!

THE JAGUAR HUNT.

[MAY, 1865.]

THE dark jaguar was abroad in the land;
   His strength and his fierceness what foe could
      withstand?
The breath of his anger was hot on the air,
And the white lamb of Peace he had dragged to his lair.

Then up rose the Farmer; he summoned his sons:
"Now saddle your horses, now look to your guns!"
And he called to his hound, as he sprang from the
      ground
To the back of his black pawing steed with a bound.

O, their hearts, at the word, how they tingled and
      stirred!
They followed, all belted and booted and spurred.
"Buckle tight, boys!" said he, "for who gallops with
      me,
Such a hunt as was never before he shall see!

" This traitor, we know him ! for when he was younger,
We flattered him, patted him, fed his fierce hunger :
But now far too long we have borne with the wrong,
For each morsel we tossed makes him savage and
    strong."

Then said one, " He must die ! " And they took up
    the cry,
" For this last crime of his he must die ! he must die ! "
But the slow eldest-born sauntered sad and forlorn,
For his heart was at home on that fair hunting-morn.

" I remember," he said, " how this fine cub we track
Has carried me many a time on his back ! "
And he called to his brothers, " Fight gently ! be
    kind ! "
And he kept the dread hound, Retribution, behind.

The dark jaguar on a bough in the brake
Crouched, silent and wily, and lithe as a snake :
They spied not their game, but, as onward they came,
Through the dense leafage gleamed two red eyeballs
    of flame.

Black-spotted, and mottled, and whiskered, and grim,
White-bellied, and yellow, he lay on the limb,
All so still that you saw but just one tawny paw
Lightly reach through the leaves and as softly withdraw.

Then shrilled his fierce cry, as the riders drew nigh,
And he shot from the bough like a bolt from the sky:
In the foremost he fastened his fangs as he fell,
While all the black jungle re-echoed his yell.

O, then there was carnage by field and by flood!
The green sod was crimsoned, the rivers ran blood,
The cornfields were trampled, and all in their track
The beautiful valley lay blasted and black.

Now the din of the conflict swells deadly and loud,
And the dust of the tumult rolls up like a cloud:
Then afar down the slope of the Southland recedes
The wild rapid clatter of galloping steeds.

With wide nostrils smoking, and flanks dripping gore,
The black stallion bore his bold rider before,
As onward they thundered through forest and glen,
A-hunting the dark jaguar to his den.

In April, sweet **April, the chase was** begun;
It was April again, **when the** hunting **was done:**
The snows of four winters and four summers green
Lay red-streaked **and trodden** and blighted between.

Then the monster **stretched all his grim length on the**
      ground;
His life-blood was wasting from **many a wound;**
Ferocious **and gory** and dying **he lay,**
Amid heaps of the whitening bones of his prey.

" **So rapine and treason** forever shall cease ! "
And they wash the stained fleece **of** the pale lamb of
      Peace;
When, lo ! **a** strong angel stands wingéd and **white**
In a wonderful raiment of ravishing light !

Peace is raised from the dead ! In the radiance shed
By the halo of glory that shines round her head,
Fair gardens shall bloom where the black jungle
      grew,   .
And **all** the glad **valley** shall blossom **anew!**

THE SWORD OF BOLIVAR.

[NOVEMBER, 1866.]

WITH the steadfast stars above us,
　　And the molten stars below,
We sailed through the Southern midnight,
　　By the coast of Mexico.

Alone, on the desolate, dark-ringed,
　　Rolling and flashing sea,
A grim old Venezuelan
　　Kept the deck with me,

And talked to me of his country,
　　And the long Spanish war,
And told how a young Republic
　　Forged the sword of Bolivar.

Of no base mundane metal
  Was the wondrous weapon made,
And in no earth-born fire
  Was fashioned the sacred blade.

But that it might shine the symbol
  Of law and light in the land,
Dropped down as a star from heaven,
  To flame in a hero's hand,

And be to the world a portent
  Of eternal might and right,
They chose for the steel a splinter
  From a fallen aerolite.

Then a virgin forge they builded
  By the city, and kindled it
With flame from a shattered palm-tree,
  Which the lightning's torch had lit, —

That no fire of earthly passion
  Might taint the holy sword,

And no ancient error tarnish
 The falchion of the Lord.

For Quito and New Granada
 And Venezuela they pour
From three crucibles the dazzling
 White meteoric ore. .

In three ingots it is moulded,
 And welded into one,
For an emblem of Colombia,
 Bright daughter of the sun!

It is drawn on a virgin anvil,
 It is heated and hammered and rolled,
It is shaped and tempered and burnished,
 And set in a hilt of gold ;

For thus by the fire and the hammer
 Of war a nation is built,
And ever the sword of its power
 Is swayed by a golden hilt.

Then with pomp and oratory
 The mustachioed señores brought
To the house of the Liberator
 The weapon they had wrought;

And they said, **in their stately** phrases,
 "O mighty in peace **and war!**
No mortal **blade** we bring **you,**
 But a flaming meteor.

"The sword **of the** Spaniard is broken,
 And to you in its stead is given,
To lead and redeem a nation,
 This ray of light from heaven."

The gaunt-faced Liberator
 From their hands the symbol took,
And waved it aloft **in** the sunlight,
 With a high, heroic look;

And he **called the saints** to witness:
 "May these lips turn into **dust,**

  5*

And this right hand fail, if ever
  It prove recreant to its trust!

" Never the sigh of a bondman
  Shall cloud this gleaming steel,
But only the foe and the traitor
  Its vengeful edge shall feel.

" Never a tear of my country
  Its purity shall stain,
Till into your hands, who gave it,
  I render it again."

Now if ever a chief was chosen
  To cover a cause with shame,
And if ever there breathed a caitiff,
  Bolivar was his name.

From his place among the people
  To the highest seat he went,
By the winding paths of party
  And the stair of accident.

A restless, weak usurper,
 Striving to rear a throne,
Filling his fame with counsels
 And conquests not his own ; —

Now seeming to put from him
 The sceptre of command,
Only that he might grasp it
 With yet a firmer hand ; —

His country's trusted leader,
 In league with his country's foes,
Stabbing the cause that nursed him,
 And openly serving those ; —

The chief of a great republic
 Plotting rebellion still, —
An apostate faithful only
 To his own ambitious will.

Drunk with a vain ambition,
 In his feeble, reckless hand,

The sword of Eternal Justice
   Became but a brawler's brand.

And Colombia was dissevered,
   Rent by factions, till at last
Her place among the nations
   Is a memory of the past.

Here the grim old Venezuelan
   Puffed fiercely his red cigar
A brief moment, then in the ocean
   It vanished like a star :

And he slumbered in his hammock ;
   And only the ceaseless rush
Of the reeling and sparkling waters
   Filled the solemn midnight hush,

As I leaned by the swinging gunwale
   Of the good ship, sailing slow,
With the steadfast heavens above her,
   And the molten heavens below.

Then I thought with sorrow and yearning
  Of my own distracted land,
And the sword let down from heaven
  To flame in her ruler's hand, —

The sword of Freedom, resplendent
  As a beam of the morning star,
Received, reviled, and dishonored
  By another than Bolivar!

LIGHTER PIECES.

IF ever there lived a Yankee lad,
 Wise or otherwise, good or bad,
Who, seeing the birds fly, did n't jump
With flapping arms from stake or stump,
  Or, spreading the tail
  Of his coat for a sail,
Take a soaring leap from post or rail,
  And wonder why
  He could n't fly,
And flap and flutter and wish and try, —
If ever you knew a country dunce
Who did n't try that as often as once,
All I can say is, that 's a sign
He never would do for a hero of mine.

An aspiring genius was D. Green:
The son of a farmer, — age fourteen;

H

His body was long and lank and lean, —
Just right for flying, as will be seen ;
He had two eyes as bright as a bean,
And a freckled nose that grew between,
A little awry, — for I must mention
That he had riveted his attention
Upon his wonderful invention,
Twisting his tongue as he twisted the strings
And working his face as he worked the wings,
And with every turn of gimlet and screw
Turning and screwing his mouth round too,
     Till his nose seemed bent .
     To catch the scent,
Around some corner, of new-baked pies,
And his wrinkled cheeks and his squinting eyes
Grew puckered into a queer grimace,
That made him look very droll in the face,
     And also very wise.

And wise he must have been, to do more
Than ever a genius did before,
Excepting Dædalus of yore

And his son **Icarus**, who wore

    Upon **their** backs

    Those wings of wax

He had **read of in** the old almanacks.

Darius was clearly **of the** opinion,

That the air was also man's **dominion,**

And that, **with** paddle or fin or pinion,

    We **soon** or late

    Should navigate

The azure **as now we** sail the sea.

The thing looks **simple** enough **to** me;

    And if you doubt it,

Hear how Darius reasoned about it.

    "The **birds** can **fly,**

    An' why can't I?

    Must **we** give in,"

    Says he with **a** grin,

    "'T the bluebird an' phœbe

    Are smarter 'n we be?

Jest fold **our** hands an' **see the swaller**

An' blackbird an' catbird beat us holler?

Doos the leetle chatterin', sassy wren,
No bigger 'n my thumb, know more than men?
    Jest show me that!
    Er prove 't the bat
Hez got more brains than 's in my hat,
An' I 'll back down, an' not till then!"

He argued further: "Ner I can't see
What 's th' use o' wings to a bumble-bee,
Fer to git a livin' with, more 'n to me; —
    Ain't my business
    Importanter 'n his'n is?

    " That Icarus
    Was a silly cuss, —
Him an' his daddy Dædalus.
They might 'a' knowed wings made o' wax
Would n't stan' sun-heat an' hard whacks.
    I 'll make mine o' luther,
    Er suthin' er other."

And he said to himself, as he tinkered and planned:
"But I ain't goin' to show my hand

To nummies that never can understand
The fust idee that 's big an' grand.
     They 'd 'a' laft an' made fun
O' Creation itself afore 't was done!"
So he kept his secret from all the rest,
Safely buttoned within his vest;
And in the loft above the shed
Himself he locks, with thimble and thread
And wax and hammer and buckles and screws,
And all such things as geniuses use; —
Two bats for patterns, curious fellows!
A charcoal-pot and a pair of bellows;
An old hoop-skirt or two, as well as
Some wire, and several old umbrellas;
A carriage-cover, for tail and wings;
A piece of harness; and straps and strings;
     And a big strong box,
       In which he locks
These and a hundred other things.

His grinning brothers, Reuben and Burke
And Nathan and Jotham and Solomon, lurk

Around the corner to see him work, —
Sitting cross-leggéd, like a Turk,
Drawing the waxed-end through with a jerk,
And boring the holes with a comical quirk
Of his wise old head, and a knowing smirk.
But vainly they mounted each other's backs,
And poked through knot-holes and pried through cracks ;
With wood from the pile and straw from the stacks
He plugged the knot-holes and calked the cracks ;
And a bucket of water, which one would think
He had brought up into the loft to drink
    When he chanced to be dry,
    Stood always nigh,
    For Darius was sly !
And whenever at work he happened to spy
At chink or crevice a blinking eye,
He let a dipper of water fly.
"Take that ! an' ef ever ye git a peep,
Guess ye 'll ketch a weasel asleep ! "
    And he sings as he locks
    His big strong box : —

SONG.

"The weasel's head is small an' trim,
An' he is leetle an' long an' slim,
An' quick of motion an' nimble of limb,
    An' ef yeou 'll be
    Advised by me,
Keep wide awake when ye 're ketchin' him !"

    So day after day
He stitched and tinkered and hammered away,
    Till at last 't was done,—
The greatest invention under the sun !
"An' now," says Darius, "hooray fer some fun !"

    'T was the Fourth of July,
    And the weather was dry,
And not a cloud was on all the sky,
Save a few light fleeces, which here and there,
    Half mist, half air,
Like foam on the ocean went floating by :

Just as lovely a morning as ever was seen
For a nice little trip in a flying-machine.

Thought cunning Darius: "Now I sha' n't go
Along 'ith the fellers to see the show.
I 'll say I 've got sich a terrible cough!
An' then, when the folks 'ave all gone off,
    I 'll hev full swing
     Fer to try the thing,
An' practyse a leetle on the wing."

"Ain't goin' to see the celebration?"
Says Brother Nate. "No; botheration!
I 've got sich a cold — a toothache — I —
My gracious! — feel 's though I should fly!"

    Said Jotham, "'Sho!
    Guess ye better go."
    But Darius said, "No!
Should n't wonder 'f yeou might see me, though,
'Long 'bout noon, ef I git red
O' this jumpin', thumpin' pain 'n my head."
For all the while to himself he said : —

"I tell ye what!
I 'll fly a few times around the lot,
To see how 't seems, then soon 's I 've got
The hang o' the thing, ez likely 's not,
    I 'll astonish the nation,
    An' all creation,
By flyin' over the celebration!
Over their heads I 'll sail like an eagle;
I 'll balance myself on my wings like a sea-gull;
I 'll dance on the chimbleys; I 'll stan' on the
    steeple;
I 'll flop up to winders an' scare the people!
I 'll light on the libbe'ty-pole, an' crow;
An' I 'll say to the gawpin' fools below,
    'What world 's this 'ere
    That I 've come near?'
Fer I 'll make 'em b'lieve I 'm a chap f'm the moon;
An' I 'll try a race 'ith their ol' bulloon!"

    He crept from his bed;
And, seeing the others were gone, he said,
"I 'm a gittin' over the cold 'n my head."

2

And away he sped,
To open the wonderful box in the shed.

His brothers had walked but a little way
When Jotham to Nathan chanced to say,
" What on airth is he up to, hey ? "
" Don'o', — the' 's suthin' er other to pay,
Er he would n't 'a' stayed to hum to-day."
Says Burke, " His toothache 's all 'n his eye !
He never 'd miss a Fo'th-o'-July,
Ef he hed n't got some machine to try."
Then Sol, the little one, spoke : " By darn !
Le 's hurry back an' hide 'n the barn,
An' pay him fer tellin' us that yarn ! "
" Agreed ! " Through the orchard they creep back,
Along by the fences, behind the stack,
And one by one, through a hole in the wall,
In under the dusty barn they crawl,
Dressed in their Sunday garments all ;
And a very astonishing sight was that,
When each in his cobwebbed coat and hat
Came up through the floor like an ancient rat

And **there** they hid ;

And Reuben slid

The fastenings **back, and the** door undid.

" Keep dark ! " **said he,**

" **While I** squint an' see what the' is to see."

As knights of **old put** on their **mail, —**

From head to foot

An iron suit,

Iron jacket and iron boot,

Iron breeches, and on the head

No hat, but an iron pot instead,

And under the chin the bail, —

I believe **they called the thing a helm ;**

And the lid they carried they called a shield ;

And, thus accoutred, they took the field,

Sallying forth to overwhelm

The dragons and pagans that plagued the realm : —

So this modern knight

Prepared **for** flight,

Put on his wings and strapped them tight ;

Jointed and jaunty, strong and **light** ;
Buckled **them fast** to shoulder and hip, —
Ten feet they measured from tip **to tip** !
And **a helm** had he, but that he wore,
Not on **his** head like those of yore,
    But more like the helm of a ship.

    " Hush ! " Reuben said,
    " He 's up in the shed !
He 's opened the winder, — I see his head !
    He stretches it out,
    An' pokes it **about,**
Lookin' to see 'f the coast is clear,
    An' nobody near ; —
Guess he don'o' who 's hid in here !
He 's riggin' a spring-board over the **sill** !
Stop laffin', Solomon ! Burke, keep still !
He 's a climbin' out now — Of all **the** things !
What 's he got **on ?** I van, it **'s** wings !
An' that 't other thing ? I vum, it **'s a** tail !
An' there he sets like **a hawk** on **a rail** !
Steppin' careful, he travels the length

Of his spring-board, and teeters to try its strength.
Now he stretches his wings, like a monstrous bat;
Peeks over his shoulder, this way an' that,
Fer to see 'f the' 's any one passin' by ;
But the' 's on'y a ca'f an' a goslin' nigh.
They turn up at him a wonderin' eye,
To see — The dragon! he 's goin' to fly!
Away he goes! Jimminy! what a jump!
     Flop — flop — an' plump

     To the ground with a thump!
Flutt'rin' an' flound'rin', all 'n a lump!"

As a demon is hurled by an angel's spear,
Heels over head, to his proper sphere, —
Heels over head, and head over heels,
Dizzily down the abyss he wheels, —
So fell Darius. Upon his crown,
In the midst of the barn-yard, he came down,
In a wonderful whirl of tangled strings,
Broken braces and broken springs,
Broken tail and broken wings,
Shooting-stars, and various things, —

Barn-yard litter of straw and chaff,
And much that was n't so sweet by half.
Away with a bellow fled the calf,
And what was that ? Did the gosling laugh?
    'T is a merry roar
    From the old barn-door,
And he hears the voice of Jotham crying,
" Say, D'rius ! how de yeou like flyin' ? "

Slowly, ruefully, where he lay,
Darius just turned and looked that way,
As he stanched his sorrowful nose with his cuff.
" Wal, I like flyin' well enough,"
He said ; "but the' ain't sich a thunderin' sight
O' fun in 't when ye come to light."

MORAL.

I just have room for the moral here :
And this is the moral, — Stick to your sphere.
Or if you insist, as you have the right,
On spreading your wings for a loftier flight,
The moral is, — Take care how you light.

WATCHING THE CROWS.

"*Caw, caw!*" — You don't say so! — "*Caw, caw!*"
    — What, once more?
Seems to me I 've heard *that* observation before,
And I wish you would *some* time begin to talk sense.
Come, I 've sat here about long enough on the fence,
And I 'd like you to tell me in confidence what
Are your present intentions regarding this lot?
Why don't you do something? or else go away?
"*Caw, caw!*" — Does that mean that they 'll go or
    they 'll stay?
While I 'm watching to learn what they 're up to, I
    see
That for similar reasons they 're just watching me!

That 's right! Now be brave, and I 'll show you
    some fun!
Just light within twenty-nine yards of my gun!

I 've hunted and hunted you all round the lot,

Now you must come here, if you want to be shot!

" Caw, caw!" — There they go again! Is n't it
    strange

How they always contrive to keep just out of range?

The scamps have been shot at so often, they know

To a rod just how far the old shot-gun will throw.

Now I 've thought how I 'll serve 'em to-morrow :
    I 'll play

The game old Jack Haskell played with 'em one
    day.

His snares would n't catch 'em, his traps would n't
    spring,

And, in spite of the very best guns he could bring

To bear on the subject, the powder he spent,

And the terriblest scarecrows his wits could invent —

Loud-clattering windmills and fluttering flags,

Straw-stuffed old codgers rigged out in his rags,

And looking quite lifelike in tail-coat and cap,

Twine stretched round the cornfield, suggesting a
    trap, —

Spite of all, — and he **did all that** ever a man did, —
They pulled his corn almost before it was planted !
Then he built **him an** ambush right out in the field,
Where **a man** could lie down at his ease, quite con-
  cealed;
But though he kept watch in **it,** day after day,
And the thieves would light on it when he was away,
And tear **up the** corn all around **it,** not once
Did a crow, young or old, show himself such **a** dunce
As to come within hail while the old man was there;
For they are the cunningest fools, I declare !
And, seeing him **enter,** they reasoned, no doubt,
That he must be **in there until he** came out !

Then, one morning, says he **to** young **Jack, " Now I**
  bet
I 've got an idee that 'll do for 'em yet !
Go **with me** down into the corn-lot to-day;
Then, when I **'m well placed** in the ambush, I 'll
  stay,
While you shoulder **your gun** and march back to the
  barn ;

For there 's this leetle notion crows never could larn :
They can't count, as I 'll show ye !" And show him
        he did !

Young Haskell went home while old Haskell lay hid.
And the crows' education had been so neglected, —
They were so poor in figures, — they never suspected,
If two had come down, and one only went back,
Then one must remain ! So, no sooner was Jack
Out of sight, than again to the field they came flocking
As thick as three rats in a little boy's stocking.
They darkened the air, and they blackened the ground ;
They came in a cloud to the windmill, and drowned
Its loudest *clack-clack* with a louder *caw-caw!*
They lit on the tail-coat, and laughed at the straw.
" By time !" says old Jack, "now I 've got ye !"
        Bang ! bang !

Blazed his short double-shooter right into the gang!
Then, picking the dead crows up out of the dirt, he
Was pleased to perceive that he 'd killed about thirty !

Now that 's just the way I 'll astonish the rascals !
I 'll set up an ambush, like old Mr. Haskell's —

"*Caw, caw!*" — You 're as knowing a bird as I know ;

But there *are* things **a little** too deep for a crow!

Just add one **to one** now, and what 's the amount ?

You 're mighty 'cute creeturs, **but,** then, **you** can't
      count !

You 'll see **if** I don't **get a shot!** Yes, I 'll borrow

Another boy somewhere and try ye to-morrow !

EVENING AT THE FARM.

OVER the hill the farm-boy goes,
  His shadow lengthens along the land,
A giant staff in a giant hand;
In the poplar-tree, above the spring,
The katydid begins to sing;
  The early dews are falling;—
Into the stone-heap darts the mink;
The swallows skim the river's brink;
And home to the woodland fly the crows,
When over the hill the farm-boy goes,
  Cheerily calling,
  "Co', boss! co', boss! co'! co'! co'!"
Farther, farther, over the hill,
Faintly calling, calling still,
  "Co', boss! co', boss! co'! co'!"

Into the yard the farmer goes,
With grateful heart, at the close of day:

Harness and chain are hung away ;
In the wagon-shed stand yoke and plough,
The straw 's in the stack, the hay in the mow
 The cooling dews are falling ; —
The friendly sheep his welcome bleat,
The pigs come grunting to his feet,
And the whinnying mare her master knows,
When into the yard the farmer goes,
 His cattle calling, —
 "Co', boss ! co', boss ! co' ! co' ! co' !"
While still the cow-boy, far away,
Goes seeking those that have gone astray, —
 "Co', boss ! co', boss ! co' ! co' !"

Now to her task the milkmaid goes.
The cattle come crowding through the gate,
Looing, pushing, little and great ;
About the trough, by the farm-yard pump,
The frolicsome yearlings frisk and jump,
 While the pleasant dews are falling ; —
The new milch heifer is quick and shy,
But the old cow waits with tranquil eye,

And the white stream into the bright pail flows,
When to her task the milkmaid goes,
     Soothingly calling,
  "So, boss! so, boss! so! so! so!"
The cheerful milkmaid takes her stool,
And sits and milks in the twilight cool,
     Saying "So! so, boss! so! so!"

To supper at last the farmer goes.
The apples are pared, the paper read,
The stories are told, then all to bed.
Without, the crickets' ceaseless song
Makes shrill the silence all night long;
     The heavy dews are falling.
The housewife's hand has turned the lock;
Drowsily ticks the kitchen clock;
The household sinks to deep repose,
But still in sleep the farm boy goes
     Singing, calling, —
  "Co', boss! co' boss! co'! co'! co'!"
And oft the milkmaid, in her dreams,
Drums in the pail with the flashing streams,
     Murmuring "So, boss! so!"

THE WILD GOOSE.

WHEN gruff winter goes, and from under his snows
 Peeps the infantine clover,
And little lambs shrink on the bleak hills of March,
And April comes smiling beneath the blue arch,
Then the forester sees from his door the wild geese
 Flying over.

Some to Winnipeg's shore; those to cold Labrador;
 Upon dark Memphremagog,
Swift flying, loud crying, these soon shall alight,
And station their sentries to guard them by night,
Or marshal their ranks to the thick-wooded banks
 Of Umbagog.

Now high in the sky, scarcely seen as they fly,
 Like the head of an arrow
Shot free from its shaft; then a dark-wingéd chain;

Or at eventide **wearily over the plain,**
Flying low, flying slow, sagging, lagging they go,
      Like a harrow.

Soon **all** have departed, save one regal-hearted
      Sad prisoner only.
No more shall he breast **the** blue ether, **or** rest
In the reeds with his mate, keeping guard by her nest, —
Never glide **by** her side **down** the green-fringéd **tide**
      Fair and lonely.

With clipped pinions, fast in a farm-yard, at last
      They have **caged the** sky-ranger,
'Mid the bustle and clucking and cackle **of flocks,**
The gossip **of** geese, and **the crowing of cocks ;**
But apart from the rest, with his **proud-curving breast,**
      Walks the **stranger.**

He refuses, with **scorn** braving hunger, the corn
      From the hands **of the givers,**
Like a prince in captivity pacing his path ;
Little pleasure he **hath in** his low, stagnant bath ;
In that green, standing pool does he think of his cool
      Northern rivers?

Far away, far away, to some lone lake or bay
    His lost comrades are thronging;
In fancy he follows; he hears their glad halloos
Round beautiful beaches, in bright plashy shallows:
And now his dark eye he turns up at the sky
    With wild longing.

He hears them all day, singing, winging their way,
    Over mountains and torrents,
To Canadian hills and their clear water-courses,
To the Ottawa's springs, to the Saguenay's sources;
And now they are going far down the broad-flowing
    Saint Lawrence.

Over grass-land and grove, searching inlet and cove,
    Speeds in dreams the wild gander!
He listens, he hastens, he screams on their track;
They hear him, they cheer him, they welcome him
    back,
They shout his proud name, and with loud clamors
    claim
    Their Commander!

Past Huron and Saginaw, far over Mackinaw,
    To lovely Itaska,
Their leader he goes; every river he knows;
They flock where the silver Saskatchawan flows,
Or sit lightly afloat upon high and remote
        Athabasca.

With his consort he leads forth their young ones, and
    feeds
    By the pleasant morasses;
He shows them the tender young crab, and the bug,
The small tented snail, and the slow mantled slug,
And laughs as they eat the soft seeds and the sweet
        Water-grasses.

But danger is coming! Lo, strutting and drumming,
    The turkey-cock charges!
The bright fancy breaks, in the farm-yard he wakes;
Nevermore he alights on the blue linkéd lakes
Of the North, or upsprings upon winnowing wings
        From their marges!

Here all the long summer abides the new-comer
    In chains ignominious,
Abandoned, companionless, far from his mate ;
But his heart is still great though dishonored his state,
And his eyes still are dreaming of glad waters gleaming
    And sinuous.

Then the rude Equinox drives before it the flocks
    Of his comrades returning ;
They sail on the gale high above the Ohio's
Broad ribbon, descending on prairies and bayous;
And again his dark eye is turned up at the sky
    With wild yearning.

As sunward they go, far below, far below,
    Coils the pale Susquehanna !
He sees them, far off in the twilight, encamp as
An army of souls upon dim, ruddy pampas;
Or at sunrise arrayed upon green everglade
    And savanna.

So year after year, as their legions appear,
    His lost state he remembers;

Wondering and wistful **he watches their** flight,

Or starts at their cries **in the** desolate night,

Dropped down **to his hearkening ear** through **the**
         darkening

         Novembers.

GREEN APPLES.

PULL down the bough, Bob! Is n't this fun?
  Now give it a shake, and — there goes one!
Now put your thumb up to the other, and see
If it is n't as mellow as mellow can be!
      I know by the stripe
      It must be ripe!
That 's one apiece for you and me.

Green, are they? Well, no matter for that.
Sit down on the grass, and we 'll have a chat;
And I 'll tell you what old Parson Bute
Said last Sunday of unripe fruit.
      " Life," says he,
      " Is a bountiful tree,
Heavily laden with beautiful fruit.

" For the youth there 's love, just streaked with red,
And great joys hanging just over his head;

Happiness, honor, and great estate,
For those who patiently work and wait; —
 Blessings," said he,
 "Of every degree,
Ripening early, and ripening late.

"Take them in season, pluck and eat,
And the fruit is wholesome, the fruit is sweet;
But, O my friends!—" Here he gave a rap
On his desk, like a regular thunder-clap,
 And made such a bang,
 Old Deacon Lang
Woke up out of his Sunday nap.

Green fruit, he said, God would not bless;
But half life's sorrow and bitterness,
Half the evil and ache and crime,
Came from tasting before their time
 The fruits Heaven sent.
 Then on he went
To his *Fourthly* and *Fifthly* : — was n't it prime?

But, I say, Bob! we fellows don't care
So much for a mouthful of apple or pear;
But what we like is the fun of the thing,
When the fresh winds blow, and the hang-birds bring
      Home grubs, and sing
      To their young ones, a-swing
In their basket-nest, tied up by its string.

I like apples in various ways:
They 're first-rate roasted before the blaze
Of a winter fire; and, O my eyes!
Are n't they nice, though, made into pies?
      I scarce ever saw
      One, cooked or raw,
That was n't good for a boy of my size!

But shake your fruit from the orchard tree,
And the tune of the brook, and the hum of the bee,
And the chipmonks chippering every minute,
And the clear sweet note of the gay little linnet,
      And the grass and the flowers,
      And the long summer hours,
And the flavor of sun and breeze, are in it.

But this is a hard one! Why did n't we
Leave them another week on the tree?
Is yours as bitter? Give us a bite!
The pulp is tough, and the seeds are white,
    And the taste of it puckers
    My mouth like a sucker's!
I vow, I believe the old parson was right!

STRAWBERRIES

LITTLE Pearl Honeydew, six years old,
　From her bright ear parted the curls of gold.
And laid her head on the strawberry-bed,
To hear what the red-cheeked berries said.

Their cheeks were blushing, their breath was sweet,
She could almost hear their little hearts beat;
And the tiniest lisping, whispering sound
That ever you heard came up from the ground.

"Little friends," she said, "I wish I knew
How it is you thrive on sun and dew!"
And this is the story the berries told
To little Pearl Honeydew, six years old.

"You wish you knew? and so do we!
But we can't tell you, unless it be
That the same kind Power that cares for you
Takes care of poor little berries too.

"Tucked up snugly, and nestled below
Our coverlid of wind-woven snow,
We peep and listen, all winter long,
For the first spring day and the bluebird's song.

"When the swallows fly home to the old brown shed
And the robins build on the bough overhead,
Then out from the mould, from the darkness and cold,
Blossom and runner and leaf unfold.

"Good children then, if they come near,
And hearken a good long while, may hear
A wonderful tramping of little feet, —
So fast we grow in the summer heat.

"Our clocks are the flowers; and they count the hours
Till we can mellow in suns and showers,
With warmth of the west-wind and heat of the south,
A ripe red berry for a ripe red mouth.

"Apple-blooms whiten, and peach-blooms fall,
And roses are gay by the garden-wall,
Ere the daisy's dial gives the sign
That we can invite little Pearl to dine.

"The days are longest, the month is June,
The year is nearing its golden noon,
The weather is fine, and our feast is spread
With a green cloth and berries red.

"Just take us betwixt your finger and thumb —
And quick, O quick! for, see! there come
Tom on all-fours, and Martin the man,
And Margaret, picking as fast as they can!

"O dear! if you only knew how it shocks
Nice berries like us to be sold by the box,
And eaten by strangers, and paid for with pelf,
You would surely take pity, and eat us yourself!"

And this is the story the small lips told
To dear Pearl Honeydew, six years old,
When she laid her head on the strawberry-bed
To hear what the red-cheeked berries said.

THE SUMMER SQUALL.

"GOODNESS gracious! what 's the matter?
  What a clamor, what a clatter!
Gracious goodness! was there ever
Such a terrible — I never!
Run and shut the chamber windows!
Jenny, keep the children in-doors!
The clothes upon the line go dancing —
Where 's the basket? Bring the pans in!
O dear!" For now the rain is coming;
You hear the chimney swallows drumming,
With a mighty fuss and flutter,
While the chimneys moan and mutter;
And see! the crumbled soot is flying
All over the pork that Jane was frying.

What a clamor, what a clatter!
The swift, slant rain begins to patter;

The geese they cackle, cow-bells rattle,
The pelted and affrighted cattle,
Across the pasture, helter-skelter,
Run to the nearest trees for shelter;
The old hen calls her skulking chickens;
The fowls fly home; the darkness thickens;
The roadside maples twist and swing,
The barn-door flaps a broken wing;
The old well-pail sets out to travel,
And drags the chain across the gravel;
In vain the farmer's wife is trying
To catch the clothes as they are flying;
Nine new tin pans are bruised and battered,
And all about the door-yard scattered;
And thicker, thicker, faster, faster,
Come tumult, tempest, and disaster.

The wind has blown the haycocks over;
The rain has spoiled the unraked clover;
With half a load the horses hurry,
And one half—flung on in the flurry,
Invisible pitchforks tearing, tossing —

Was blown into the creek in crossing;
And thicker, thicker, faster, faster,
Come whirlwind, tempest, and disaster.

Now, all without the storm is roaring,
The house is shut, the rain is pouring;
Incessantly its fury lashes
The roof, the clapboards, and the sashes;
The fowls have gone to roost at noon,
We 'll have the candles lighted soon.
In flies the door, — the farmer enters
Dripping and drenching from his adventures;
Finds Jenny sighing, baby crying,
The frightened children hushed, and lying
Huddled upon the bed together;
Mother storming, like the weather;
With pans, and chairs, and baskets, which in
Wet confusion crowd the kitchen.

But Hugh is not the man to grieve;
He shakes his hat, and strokes his sleeve,
And laughs, and jests, and wrings his blouse: —

His very presence in the house
Dispels like sunshine the bewildering
And awful gloom that wrapped the children.
Old Farmer Hugh! the whole world through,
I find no nobler soul than you!
A heart to welcome every comer,
Alike the Winter and the Summer.
When Fortune, with her fickle chances,
Now smiles, now frowns, retreats, advances,
To make poor mortals mourn the loss of her,
You, trustful heart and true philosopher,
Securely centred in your station,
Yourself the pivot of gyration,
Look forth serenely patient, seeing
All things come round to your true being.

O thus, like you, when sudden squalls
Of angry fortune strike my walls,
Spoil expectation's unraked clover,
And blow my hopes like haycocks over, —
When storm and darkness, wild, uncertain,
Deluge my sky with their black curtain, —

O then, like you, brave Farmer Hugh!
May I, with vision clear and true,
Behold, beyond each transient sorrow,
The gleam and gladness of to-morrow.

CORN HARVEST.

THE fields are filled with a smoky haze.
      The golden spears
      Of the ripening ears
Peep from the crested and pennoned maize.
All down the rustling rows are rolled
The portly pumpkins, green and gold.
        Altogether
        'T is very fine weather,
Just as the almanac foretold.

In early summer the brigand crow
      Made ruthless raids
      On the sprouting blades;
The weeds fought long with the farmer's hoe;
And the raccoons and squirrels have had their share
Of all but the good man's toil and care; —
      The shy field-mouse
      Has filled her house,
And the blackbirds are flocking from no one knows
        where.

7 *

But now his time has come : hurrah !

      To the field, lads! to-day ·

      Our work will be play.

Let the blackbirds scream, and the mad crows caw,

And the squirrels scold on the wild-cherry limb, —

We 'll take from the robbers that took from him !

      Come along, one and all, boys !

      Big boys and small boys,

Long-armed Amos, and Joel, and Jim !

Bring sickles to reap, or blades to strike.

      Before they have lost

      In sun and frost

The nourishing juices the cattle like,

Sucker and stalk must be cut from the hill ;

Surround them, and bend them, then hit with a will !

      Left standing too long,

      They grow woody and strong ;

The corn in the stook will ripen still.

Carry your stroke, lads, close to the ground.

      Set the stalks upright,

      And pack them tight

In pyramids shapely and stately and round.
Give the old lady's skirts a genteel spread ;
Slope well the shoulders, so as to shed

     The autumn rain

     From the unhusked grain,

Then twist a wisp for the queer little head.

There she is, waiting to be embraced!

     Reach round her who can?

     'T will take a man

And a boy, at least, to clasp her waist!
Was ever a hug like that? Now draw
Tightly the girdle of good oat-straw!

     With the plumpest waist

     That ever was laced,

Goes the narrowest nightcap ever you saw.

We bind the corn, and leave it snug,

     Or rest in the shade

     Of the shocks we have made,

To eat our luncheon, and drink from the jug.
The children come bringing the bands, or play
Hide-and-go-seek in the corn all day,

And now and then race
With a chipmonk, or chase
A scared little field-mouse scampering away.

All day we cut and bind; till at night, —
Where a field of corn in
The misty morning
Waved, in the level September light, —
All over the shadowy stubble-land,
The stooks, like Indian wigwams, stand.
Compact and secure,
There leave them to cure,
Till the merry husking-time is at hand.

Then the fodder will be to stack or to house,
And the ears to husk.
But now the dusk
Falls soft as the shadows of cool pine-boughs;
Our good day's work is done; the night
Brings wholesome fatigue and appetite;
Up comes the balloon
Of the huge red moon,
And home we go, singing gay songs by its light.

THE LITTLE THEATRE.

I KNOW a little theatre
   Scarce bigger than a nut.
Finer than pearl its portals are,
Quick as the twinkling of a star
   They open and they shut.

A fairy palace beams within:
   So wonderful it is,
No words can tell you of its worth,—
No architect in all the earth
   Could build a house like this.

A beautiful rose window lets
   A ray into the hall;
To shade the scene from too much light,
A tiny curtain hangs in sight,
   Within the crystal wall.

And O the wonders there beside!
  The curious furniture,
The stage, with all its small machinery,
Pulley and cord and shifting scenery,
  In marvellous miniature!

A little, busy, moving world,
  It mimics space and time,
The marriage-feast, the funeral,
Old men and little children, all
  In perfect pantomime.

There pours the foaming cataract,
  There speeds the train of cars;
Day comes with all its pageantry
Of cloud and mountain, sky and sea,
  The night, with all its stars.

Ships sail upon that mimic sea;
  And smallest things that fly,
The humming-bird, the sunlit mote
Upon its golden wings afloat,
  Are mirrored in that sky.

Quick as the twinkling of the doors,
   The scenery forms or fades;
And all the fairy folk that dwell
Within the arched and windowed shell
   Are momentary shades.

Who has this wonder holds **it dear**
   As his own life and limb;
Who lacks it, not the rarest gem
That ever flashed in diadem
   Can purchase **it for him.**

Ah, then, dear picture-loving child,
   How **doubly** blessed **art thou!**
Since thine the happy fortune is
To have two little worlds like this
   In thy possession now, —

Each furnished with soft folding-doors,
   A curtain, and **a** stage!
And now a laughing sprite transfers
Into those little theatres
   The letters of this page.

THE CHARCOALMAN.

I.

THOUGH rudely blows the **wintry blast,**
And sifting snows fall white and **fast,**
Mark Haley drives along the street,
Perched high upon his wagon seat;
His sombre **face** the storm **defies,**
And thus from morn till eve **he cries,**
"Charco'! charco'!"
While echo faint and far **replies,**
"Hark, O! hark, O!"
"Charco'!"—"Hark, O!"—Such **cheery sounds**
Attend him on his daily rounds.

II.

The dust begrimes **his** ancient hat;
His coat is darker far **than that;**
'T is odd to see his sooty form
All speckled with the feathery storm;
Yet in his honest **bosom** lies

Nor spot nor speck, though still he cries,
  " Charco'! charco'!"
While many a roguish lad replies,
  " Ark, ho! ark, ho!"
" Charco'!" — " Ark, ho!" — Such various sounds
Announce Mark Haley's morning rounds.

III.

Thus all the cold and wintry day
He labors much for little pay ;
Yet feels no less of happiness
Than many a richer man, I guess,
When through the shades of eve he spies
The light of his own home, and cries,
  " Charco'! charco'!"
And Martha from the door replies,
  " Mark, ho! Mark, ho!"
" Charco'!" — " Mark, ho!" — Such joy abounds
When he has closed his daily rounds!

IV.

The hearth is warm, the fire is bright ;
And while his hand, washed clean and white,

K

Holds Martha's tender hand once more,
His glowing face bends fondly o'er
The crib wherein his darling lies,
And in a coaxing tone he cries,
     " Charco'! charco'! "
And baby with a laugh replies,
     "Ah, go! ah, go!"
" Charco'! " — " Ah, go! " — while at the sounds
The mother's heart with gladness bounds.

V.

Then honored be the charcoalman,
Though dusky as an African!
'T is not for you that chance to be
A little better clad than he
His honest manhood to despise, —
Although from morn till eve he cries,
     " Charco'! charco'! "
While mocking echo still replies,
     " Hark, O! hark, O! "
" Charco'! " — " Hark, O! " — Long may the sounds
Proclaim Mark Haley's daily rounds!

THE WONDERFUL SACK.

THE apple-boughs **half hid** the house
　　Where lived the lonely widow;
Behind it stood the chestnut wood,
　Before it spread the meadow.

She had no money in her till,
　She was too poor to borrow;
With her lame leg she could not beg;
　And no one cheered her sorrow.

Her best **black** gown was faded brown,
　Her shoes were all in tatters,
With not a pair for Sunday wear:
　Said she, "It little matters!

"**Nobody** asks me now to ride,
　My garments are not fitting;
And with my crutch I care not much
　To hobble **off** to meeting.

" I still preserve my Testament,
  And though the *Acts* are missing,
And *Luke* is torn, and *Hebrews* worn,
  On Sunday 't is a blessing.

" And other days I open it
  Before me on the table,
And there I sit, and read, and knit,
  As long as I am able."

One evening she had closed the book,
  But still she sat there knitting ;
" Meow-meow ! " complained the old·black cat ;
  " Mew-mew ! " the spotted kitten.

And on the hearth, with sober mirth,
  " Chirp, chirp ! " replied the cricket.
'T was dark, — but hark ! " Bow-ow ! " the bark
  Of Ranger at the wicket !

Is Ranger barking at the moon ?
  Or what can be the matter ?
What trouble now ? " Bow-ow ! bow-ow ! " —
  She hears the old gate clatter.

"It is the wind that bangs the gate,
　And I must knit my stocking!"
But hush!—what's that? Rat-tat! rat-tat!
　Alas! there's some one knocking!

"Dear me! dear me! who can it be?
　Where, where is my crutch-handle?"
She rubs a match with hasty scratch;
　She cannot light the candle!

Rat-tat! scratch, scratch! the worthless match!
　The cat growls in the corner.
Rat-tat! scratch, scratch! Up flies the latch,—
　"Good evening, Mrs. Warner!"

Blue burns at last the tardy match,
　And dim the candle glimmers;
Along the floor beside the door
　The cold white moonlight shimmers.

The old cat's tail ruffs big and black,
　Loud barks the old dog Ranger;
The kitten spits and lifts her back,
　Her eyes glare on the stranger.

His limbs are strong, his **beard is long,**
　　His **hair** is **dark** and wavy ;
Upon his back he bears a sack ;
　　His staff is stout and heavy.

" My way is lost, and with the frost
　　I feel my fingers tingle."
Then from his back he slips the **sack,** —
　　Ho! did you hear it jingle ?

" **Nay,** keep your chair ! while you sit **there,**
　　I 'll take the other corner."
" I 'm sorry, sir, I have no fire."
　　" No matter, Mrs. **Warner."**

He shakes his sack, — the magic sack !
　　Amazed the widow gazes :
Ho, **ho! the** chimney 's full of wood !
　　Ha, ha! the wood it blazes !

Ho, **ho!** ha, ha! the merry fire !
　　It sputters and it crackles !
Snap, snap! flash, flash! old oak **and ash**
　　Send out a million sparkles.

The stranger sits upon his sack
  Beside the chimney-corner,
And rubs his hands before the brands,
  And smiles on Mrs. Warner.

She feels her heart beat fast with fear,
  But what can be the danger?
"Can I do aught for you, kind sir?"
  "I 'm hungry," quoth the stranger.

"Alas!" she said, "I have no food
  For boiling or for baking!"
"I 've food," quoth he, "for you and me";
  And gave his sack **a** shaking.

Out rattled knives, and forks, and spoons,
  Twelve eggs, potatoes plenty,
One large soup-dish, two plates of fish,
  And bread enough for twenty.

And Rachel, calming her surprise,
  As **well as** she was able,
Saw, following these, **two** roasted geese,
  A tea-urn, and a table.

Strange, was it not? each dish was hot,
  Not even a plate was broken;
The cloth was laid, and all arrayed,
  Before a word was spoken.

"Sit up! sit up! and we will sup,
  Dear madam, while we 're able."
Said she, " The room is poor and small
  For such a famous table."

Again the stranger shakes the sack,
  The walls begin to rumble;
Another shake! the rafters quake!
  You 'd think the roof would tumble.

Shake, shake! the room grows high and large,
  The walls are painted over;
Shake, shake! out fall four chairs, in all,
  A bureau, and a sofa.

The stranger stops to wipe the drops
  That down his face are streaming.
"Sit up! sit up! and we will sup,"
  Quoth he, " while all is steaming."

The widow hobbled on her crutch,
　He kindly sprang to aid her.
"All this," said she, "is too much for me!"
　Quoth he, "We 'll have a waiter."

Shake, shake, once more! and from the sack
　Out popped a little fellow,
With elbows bare, bright eyes, sleek hair,
　And trousers striped with yellow.

His legs were short, his body plump,
　His cheek was like a cherry;
He turned three times; he gave a jump;
　His laugh rang loud and merry.

He placed his hand upon his heart,
　And scraped and bowed so handy!
"Your humble servant, sir," he said,
　Like any little dandy.

The widow laughed a long, loud laugh,
　And up she started, screaming;
When ho! and lo! the room was dark!—
　She 'd been asleep and dreaming!
　　8

The stranger and his **magic sack,**
  The dishes and **the fishes,**
The geese **and** things, had taken wings,
  Like riches, or like witches!

All, all was gone! She sat alone;
  Her hands had dropped their knitting.
" Meow-meow ! " the cat upon the mat;
  " Mew-mew ! mew-mew ! " the kitten.

The hearth is **bleak,** — **and** hark! the **creak,** —
  "Chirp, chirp!" the lonesome cricket.
" Bow-ow ! " **says** Ranger to the moon;
  The wind is at the wicket.

And still she sits, and **as she knits**
  She ponders o'er the vision :
"I **saw it** written on **the** sack, —
  'A Cheerful Disposition.'

"I know **God** sent the dream, **and meant**
  To teach this useful lesson,
That out of peace and pure content
  Springs every earthly blessing."

Said she, " I 'll make the sack my own !
   I 'll shake away all sorrow ! "
She shook the sack for me to-day ;
   She 'll shake for you to-morrow.

She shakes out hope ; and joy, and peace,
   And happiness come after ;
She shakes out smiles for all the world ;
   She shakes out love and laughter.

For poor and rich, — no matter which, —
   For young folks or for old folks,
For strong and weak, for proud and meek,
   For warm folks and for cold folks ;

For children coming home from school,
   And sometimes for the teacher ;
For white and black she shakes the sack, —
   In short, for every creature.

And everybody who has grief,
   The sufferer and the mourner,
From far and near, come now to hear
   Kind words from Mrs. Warner.

They go to her with heavy hearts,
  They come away with light ones ;
They go to her with cloudy brows,
  They come away with bright ones.

All love her well, and I could tell
  Of many a cheering present
Of fruits and things their friendship brings,
  To make her fireside pleasant.

She always keeps a cheery fire ;
  The house is painted over ; .
She has food in store, and chairs for four,
  A bureau, and a sofa.

She says these seem just like her dream,
  And tells again the vision :
" I saw it written on the sack, —
  'A Cheerful Disposition ! ' "

THE END.

Cambridge : Stereotyped and Printed by Welch, Bigelow, & Co.